Scout

The Haunted Castle

For Dexter,
This is book 2 of
a series we hope
you & Mylo will
enjoy reading!

Some little "adventures"
to go on in your
imagination :)

With love,
Opa & Oma

Scout

The Haunted Castle

by Piet Prins

INHERITANCE PUBLICATIONS
NEERLANDIA, ALBERTA, CANADA
PELLA, IOWA, U.S.A.

Library and Archives Canada Cataloguing in Publication
Prins, Piet, 1909-1985.
The haunted castle / Piet Prins.
(Scout)
Translation of: Snuf en het spookslot.
ISBN 1-894666-44-5

1. Dogs—Juvenile fiction. I. Title. II. Series: Prins, Piet, 1909-1985. Scout.
PT5866.P75S6213 2006 j839.31'364 C2006-900430-7

Library of Congress Cataloging-in-Publication Data
Prins, Piet, 1909-1985.
[Snuf en het spookslot. English]
The haunted castle / by Piet Prins.
p. cm. — (Scout)
Summary: Not long after the end of World War II, on a farm in the Netherlands, Tom, his friends, and Scout aid police and customs officials in tracking down a gang of smuggglers and solving the mystery of a nearby haunted castle.
ISBN 1-894666-44-5 (pbk.)
[1. Smugglers—Fiction. 2. Castles—Fiction. 3. Dogs—Fiction. 4. Netherlands—History—German occupation, 1940-1945—Fiction. 5. Mystery and detective stories.] I. Title.
PZ7.P9366Hau 2006
[Fic]—dc22

2005037013

ISBN 978-1-894666-44-2

Originally published as *Snuf en het Spookslot*

Cover and illustrations by Jaap Kramer

4th Pinting 2020

Inheritance Publications
3317 Township Rd 624
County of Barrhead, AB T0G 1R1 Canada
Tel. 780-674-3949
Web site: inhpubl.net
E-Mail: orders@inhpubl.net

Printed in Canada

Contents

Books by Piet Prins

Scout Series:
The Secret of the Swamp
The Haunted Castle
The Flying Phantom
The Sailing Sleuths
The Treasure of Rodensteyn Castle
The Mystery of the Abandoned Mill
Scout's Distant Journey

Anak, the Eskimo Boy

The Four Adventurers - The Evil Professor
Four Adventurers - The Mystery of the Three Fingered Villain

Run Kevin, Run!

Shadow 1 - The Lonely Sentinel
Shadow 2 - Hideout in the Swamp
Shadow 3 - The Grim Reaper
Shadow 4 - The Partisans
Shadow 5 - Sabotage

Sheltie 1 - The Curse of Urumbu
Sheltie 2 -The Search for Sheltie

Stefan Derksen's Polar Adventure

Struggle 1 - When the Morning Came
Struggle 2 - Dispelling the Tyranny
Struggle 3 - The Beggars' Victory

Wambu 1 - The Chieftain's Son
Wambu 2 - In the Valley of Death
Wambu 3 - Journey to Manhood

CHAPTER I

A Stray Arrow

Cycling down the village street came a young boy. He was flying along on a brand new bicycle which had been his for only two days. Beside him ran a strong, beautiful German shepherd. He kept up to his young master with a long, loping, tireless stride.

The boy was Tom Sanders. The dog was called Scout. The two had been inseparable friends for several years now. Tom had gotten Scout as a very young puppy. The boy and the dog had experienced some hair-raising adventures together during the Second World War and the German occupation of the Netherlands. Both had almost lost their lives on several occasions, but they had come through all right. It was now about a year since the town where Tom lived had been liberated by the Allies. Many things had happened in that time. There was plenty of food again. Most items were no longer rationed, but available to everyone. Yet the best was that everyone was free again. Nobody had to be afraid anymore to be picked up by the secret police and to end up in a concentration camp, or to be shot.

The newspapers could appear freely again and didn't have to be filled with lies of the Germans. The ministers did not have to be afraid anymore that they would be picked up if they prayed for the Queen on Sundays. The Queen was back in the country, and with her liberty had returned.

Last week Tom had celebrated his birthday and received a new bike. His old one had become a rusty rattletrap during the war, so he was very happy with his gift.

Arriving at the outskirts of the village, Tom slowed down a little. Scout could keep up this pace for a long time, but Tom didn't want to hurt his dog.

A kilometre or so farther down the road stood a large windmill and next to it, a sawmill and a house, in which lived the Van Doorn family. Carl van Doorn was one of Tom's two best friends.

The other friend, Bert Verhoef, lived on a farm even farther from town.

Tom didn't have any homework tonight and was on his way to Carl's house. There was always something to do around the windmill and the lumber yard. Maybe Bert would be there too, if he wasn't too busy at the farm.

Tom coasted onto the yard in front of the mill, whistling a few notes that the three friends used as a signal. The whistle came back to him from high in the sky. He looked up and spotted Carl and Bert waving at him from a small window just under the crown of the windmill.

"Come on up, Man! It's really nice up here!" shouted Bert.

Tom parked his bike, ran inside through the open door of the mill and quickly climbed to the top. Scout barked indignantly because he had to stay behind. In the top of the windmill was a small room from which you could view the whole surrounding countryside through two narrow little windows. In the last days of the war the boys had used this place as a lookout.

Tom got an enthusiastic welcome. Carl proudly showed Tom something he had just finished making: a long, powerful bow, strung and ready to shoot. He had also made six arrows.

"It shoots a long ways!" he told Tom. "Bert and I have been practising in the yard. Now we're going to try it from here. Then it will shoot even farther!"

"Wow! Do I get a turn too? I think I can shoot farther than either of you."

"Brag, brag," taunted Bert. "Let's teach him a lesson."

Carl took charge. "We'll have a contest. Each of us gets two arrows. First we'll take one arrow and see who can shoot the farthest from the window in the back. That way we'll have the wind with us. Watch closely where the arrows land, because we'll have to find them pretty soon."

Tom shot first. He pulled the string back as far as it would go. The arrow whizzed away in a blur of speed, landing in the field far beyond the rear yard.

"Not bad for an amateur! Now give the bow to a master archer," said Bert, "and let me show you how an expert does it."

Tom had a reply on the tip of his tongue, but he said nothing. First he would see how the "master archer" fared. Bert seemed to know what he was doing, for the arrow he shot went quite a few metres farther than Tom's.

Now it was Carl's turn. He, too, succeeded in getting his arrow past Tom's.

"First prize, Bert Verhoef! Second prize, Carl van Doorn! Consolation prize, Tom Sanders!" Carl bugled ceremoniously. Then he went on in a normal voice, "The contest isn't finished yet. Now we'll see who can shoot the straightest."

He went to the other window, which looked down on the house. For a moment he looked around for a good target. Ha, something caught his eye. "Okay, you boys. See where the eaves trough widens just above the drainpipe? That's what we'll aim for."

Tom was again allowed to go first. This was it. He couldn't allow his friends to show him up again. The target was quite far away and rather small. He aimed down very carefully.

He released the arrow . . . "Bullseye!" shouted Tom at the same time that he heard a hollow plunk, as the dull tip of the arrow struck the metal gutter.

Bert kept his wisecracks to himself this time. This shot was going to be hard to beat. His arrow landed on the roof, more than a metre from its target.

"You're too far to the left," remarked Carl. "Tom had the right idea, but he didn't hit it dead centre. I'll show you boys how it's done."

As his companions looked on attentively and critically, he released the arrow. At the same moment the three boys gasped in shock. Around the corner of the house came a gentleman dressed in black and wearing a tophat. In his eagerness to better Bert's bad shot and even surpass Tom's, Carl had aimed too far to the right. The arrow flashed straight toward the visitor, who came on completely unawares. For a second it looked like he was going to be hit right in the face. But they were fortunate. The arrow struck the man's tophat. Gracefully the hat sailed to the ground, where a playful gust of wind ran off with it, rolling it around the yard.

The man was startled, but a second later he valorously charged forward to rescue his proud head covering. He galloped after the hat, which tumbled from one corner of the yard to the other. The man's long coattails fluttered behind him like startled crows, his gray mop of hair flip-flopped wildly and his ruddy face turned even redder. After a few moments he had captured the fugitive hat and tried to clean it off with a big, red handkerchief, but he didn't seem to have much success. Then he looked around to see who had done this dastardly deed. He looked at the windmill but didn't see his abuser, for Carl and his friends had ducked just in the nick of time.

Since the stray arrow had done no real damage, Tom and Bert were choking with laughter. But Carl saw nothing funny in the whole situation.

"That's my Uncle Klaus," he said glumly. "He's my mother's favourite brother. He doesn't come very often because he lives far away, on a farm close to the German border. I'm afraid we ruined his hat. Now I'm afraid to go in and meet him."

Carefully Tom took a quick peek through the little window. The door of the house opened and out came Carl's father.

"Klaus! What a surprise! And dressed so formally! You look like a preacher."

Uncle Klaus stopped trying to clean his hat. "Yes, I'd sooner be wearing my coveralls, but I had to go to a funeral not far from here — a niece of mine by marriage. So I thought I'd stop by and look in on you, but I got a rather strange reception."

"What do you mean?" Van Doorn asked, puzzled.

"Well, I came around the corner of the house and suddenly something hit my topper. It rolled around on the ground, which didn't do it any good, I'm afraid. But, anyway, what's a farmer doing wearing a stovepipe hat anyway!"

Van Doorn spotted one of the arrows lying in the yard and immediately guessed what had happened. "I'll find the guilty party in a minute," he said darkly, "and somebody's going to wish he were somewhere else. Come on in."

They disappeared inside. The three friends in the windmill had heard every word that was said. Ruefully they looked at each other. Things didn't look very good for Carl.

"I guess the best thing to do is to go into the house and fess up," muttered Carl. "After all, I didn't do it on purpose."

The others agreed, but they weren't about to let him take the punishment alone. They had also participated in the dangerous contest, and it could just as well have been one of them who had shot the arrow. They agreed they would go together, but no one made a move toward the ladder.

Then suddenly the loud, clear tone of a bell sounded.

"That's the signal for coffee time," said Carl. "We can't put it off any longer. Let' s go."

They climbed down the long ladder to the bottom of the windmill. Downstairs they were greeted by Scout, who leaped up against them in excitement. Carl put away the bow. The arrows they would pick up later.

Timidly the threesome entered the house, followed by the frolicking dog.

"Here are our sharpshooters!" cried Uncle Klaus. To the boys' relief, he no longer looked angry. The boys shook hands with the visitor and mumbled their names. The name of Carl's uncle was Wentinck. Mr. van Doorn was holding the arrow in his hand and stared with raised eyebrows at the three boys, who had already betrayed their guilt by their bashful behaviour.

Carl overcame his reluctance and said, "I'm very sorry about the arrow, Uncle Klaus. I shot it, but I had no idea anyone was coming around the house."

"I don't know: it seems to me you hit the bullseye dead centre," teased Wentinck. "After you get a little practice, there won't be a man in town who feels safe in his tophat."

Carl blushed bright red. His companions tried to help him by shouldering some of the blame. Uncle Klaus, however, wasn't really angry; he was just in a teasing mood. His remarks made the boys tongue-tied. Van Doorn looked on, grinning broadly.

Fortunately a few moments later Carl's mother came in carrying the abused hat. "It's all right," she assured him. "You can't even find the spot where the arrow hit it."

"Well done," Wentinck praised her, turning the hat in his hands. "Thanks a lot. And now let's bury it. Not the hat, but the whole matter. I've teased these boys enough. Pretty soon they'll think I'm nothing but an old bear."

"Oh, I know better than that, Uncle Klaus," said Carl, laughing with relief. Tom and Bert, too, saw that the old farmer wasn't one to hold a grudge.

As they had their coffee, Wentinck chatted amiably about his family, about his farm, and about the area of the country where he lived — an exceptionally beautiful stretch of country that had not yet been discovered by the tourist industry.

After a while, the talk strayed back to the years of the German occupation. Wentinck had already heard a little about what had happened in the village during those days. Van Doorn told him how he had been imprisoned by the Germans and rescued by the three boys. Along with Scout, the three friends had carried themselves very bravely, providing important help to the Allies during the liberation of the village. Gradually Wentinck began to get a much different impression of the three boys. He studied them with new respect: there was more to them than met the eye.

Finally Bert said it was time for him to go home. He had to get up early the next morning to do his work on the farm. Tom, too, stood up to leave.

As they said goodnight, Wentinck said, "If you fellows would like to spend a couple of weeks at our place this summer, let me know. I've got plenty of room, and it's an ideal area to spend a vacation."

"You mean all three of us, Uncle Klaus?" Carl asked in surprise.

Wentinck shook his head. "No, you misunderstood me."

Looking at the boys' disappointed faces, he added with a little grin, "I meant all four of you. Scout seems to be part of the gang too."

"Whoopee!" shouted Tom enthusiastically. "Thanks, Mr. Wentinck!"

Carl, too, leaped at the invitation. Bert alone hesitated. He would love to go, but he was needed at home on the farm. He wasn't sure his father could afford to let him go during the summer.

Wentinck clapped him on the shoulder encouragingly. "You'll have to come along too. It's important for a future farmer who really wants to learn his trade to get acquainted with another farm than your own for a change. I'm sure you'll pick up something that will be useful to you later on. Just tell your father that I said so."

Carl walked his friends home a little ways. He had spent time at Uncle Klaus's farm before, and he gave his friends a glowing description of the fun he had had and of how beautiful the countryside was. The three of them would have a wonderful time.

"If only my dad lets me go!" sighed Bert. "At least your uncle gave me a good argument to use on him. I'll try it out tonight."

They parted, promising to meet again in two days to find out how they had fared.

Two days later an exceedingly happy Bert told them he had been given permission to go. His father had looked doubtful at first, but then had given in quite easily.

Tom had also had some trouble, but of quite a different sort. His younger sister Ina and also Miriam, the young Jewish girl adopted by the Sanders, had been extremely jealous and had been badgering him without letup, because they, too, wanted to come along. Tom had, of course, told them, "Not a chance!"

But when he told Carl about the girls, he said, "Oh, I don't know. My uncle and aunt like lots of guests around, and they have plenty of room. I'll ask my father and mother and see what they think. If they think it's okay, I'll write Uncle Klaus a letter to ask him if the girls are also welcome."

A week later the letter was sent out and three days later came the reply, in the form of an enthusiastic invitation to Ina and Miriam. The girls were tremendously happy, and now all of the young people were eagerly looking forward to the summer vacation, which promised to be an exceptionally exciting one.

CHAPTER II

The Valley

The train noisily steamed into the small station in a small farming town not far from the German border. The brakes squealed and the huge machine ground to a halt, still huffing and puffing. Several doors opened and a few passengers stepped out.

Usually this station was not very busy. But this time was an exception. From one of the coaches spilled a noisy party of two girls and three boys, followed by a large German shepherd with a handsome, intelligent face. Chatting and laughing, they trooped across the platform toward the exit, lugging along their baggage consisting of several suitcases and backpacks.

It was Carl van Doorn and his two friends, and Ina and Miriam. The dog, of course, was Scout, Tom's inseparable companion. The party passed through the checkout and emerged in the village square, which was overshadowed by huge, old trees. For a moment they stood together looking around.

"I don't see anybody," said Carl. "My cousin was supposed to be here to pick us up."

Shading his eyes with his hand, he peered down the long street that led into the square. The road was bright with the glare of the sun, for it was mid-summer. But the person Carl was looking for was nowhere to be seen.

The group shuffled about indecisively, not knowing what to do.

Suddenly a loud laugh sounded behind them. They turned around and saw a young man about eighteen years old with a deeply tanned face and dark, unruly hair. He stepped toward Carl and shook hands with him.

"You were looking the wrong way, Cousin. I was here all the time, but I parked my horse and wagon on the other side, under the trees where it's nice and cool. My horse was hot from the trip down here, and he's going to be hauling quite a load on the way back."

Then he greeted the others. "Hi, my name is Jake," he said, shaking hands all around. "I'm afraid I don't know your names, except for Scout. Him I have heard about."

The youngsters laughed and gave him their names. Jake looked like a nice enough fellow.

Together they walked to the corner of the square where Jake had tied his horse to a tree. The horse was a tall, long-legged animal with a beautifully shaped head. He was hitched to a light, four-wheeled wagon.

"Climb aboard," said Jake. "We'll leave right away."

Everyone found a spot in the wagon in short order. Scout too jumped aboard. Carl sat next to his cousin on the seat. Jake tapped the horse with the reins and the animal immediately broke into a trot.

The group enjoyed the ride tremendously. The scenery here was much different from that around their village. First they rode through a rather flat stretch of land, where they saw old Saxon farmhouses still standing here and there. But gradually they entered hillier terrain. Finally the wagon turned down a narrow country

road that led through a dense woods. In some places the trees overhung the road like a green canopy, so although it was midday they were riding through a mysterious gloom. Farther on it again became lighter.

Now they were riding up a rather steep incline. The horse moved on step by step, for it was no easy job pulling a wagon load of young people up the hill.

When they reached the top, they had a magnificent view of a picturesque valley that lay before them. In a blue haze in the distance they saw other hills that were even higher and steeper.

"Boy, is it ever beautiful!" said Tom. "Tomorrow we'll have to take a hike to those big hills yonder."

"I don't think so," said Jake, laughing. "They're in Germany, and well before you got there you'd have been picked up by the border police, because you're not even allowed close to the border."

Now they were going downhill at a fast clip. The group thought it was great fun. Bert and Tom were standing up, but Tom wasn't used to riding in a wagon and had trouble keeping his balance on the bouncing wagon.

Scout had jumped out and was running alongside the vehicle barking excitedly. Suddenly Jake turned the horse off to the right onto a small dirt road. On one side were woods and on the other side farmland. The wagon was now going much slower. The dirt lane took several turns, sometimes passing through tall woods and sometimes through open country. Suddenly, ahead of them in a small valley they saw a lovely, stately farmhouse.

The young people were filled with excitement when Jake told them that this was his father's farm. Only Carl had been here before.

"It's beautiful!" sighed Ina, enthralled. And Miriam too was deeply impressed.

They all jumped down from the wagon, except Jake who had to stable the horse. Running, the group made for the farmhouse. When they arrived on the yard, Mr. Wentinck was just coming out of the barn.

"So, here are our house guests!" he said as he approached them. "Come right inside. I think you might be thirsty in this heat."

Meanwhile, Jake had also driven onto the yard, so the young vacationers unloaded their suitcases and backpacks from the wagon and trooped into the house. They stepped into a huge room with a stone-tiled floor. Along the wall stood two heavy wooden cabinets loaded with shiny copper houseware, and on one end of the room was a large fireplace decorated with blue tiles. In the far corner stood a tall grandfather's clock. The children stared wide-eyed, dazzled by all the pretty things.

Mrs. Wentinck and Hanna (Jake's older sister) gave them a warm welcome. Everyone received a big glass of buttermilk. Then Hanna took the guests along to show them where they would be sleeping.

Ina and Miriam were led to a cozy little room up in the attic. It had a window that swung open and gave them a splendid view of the surrounding countryside. The boys would be staying in one of the outbuildings on the farm. On the second floor of one of his barns, Mr. Wentinck had fixed up a good-sized room with several beds. It was used quite often by city people who wanted to vacation in this area.

In the meantime, evening had stolen up on them. The day's heat was beginning to lift, but it was still completely light outside. The young people wanted to look around the farm a little more, and Mrs. Wentinck said they still had plenty of time before bedtime. Jake went along to act as their tour guide.

Even in the yard there were many things to see. Carl, who was very interested in electricity and machines, walked toward one of the small buildings where he saw a large number of big batteries.

"What's that?" he asked Jake.

Jake put on an air of mystery. "That's our own power station," he said importantly. "We don't just can fruit and vegetables, we also can electricity. The power is collected in these big batteries. They keep our lights burning at night."

He walked to a switch on the wall of the shed and turned it. An electric light came on.

But Carl wasn't satisfied. "Where do you get your power?" he asked. Jake laughed. "I'll show you pretty soon. Just wait and see: there are all kinds of things around here that you've never seen in town," he said.

They strolled on, passing several stacks of beehives which were still humming with activity as the industrious honey bees returned with their last load of nectar. The girls had misgivings about going so close, but Jake assured them that they need not be afraid as long as they moved calmly.

There were many other things to see. Along the garden were several old trees, among them a couple of chestnut trees loaded with nuts. Tom was going to pick a few nuts off a low-hanging branch, but the long spines scared him off.

"We'd better hurry up," said Jake. "You can look around here all you want in the next few days, but I'd like to go into the woods for a little while yet."

Chatting happily, they followed their guide and were soon within the dense woods. Along the path flowed a swift stream of crystal-clear water. It was very quiet in the woods. The birds were still singing their melodies, but all other daytime sounds seemed to have been stilled. From far away, however, came a strange roaring, rumbling sound that none of them could identify.

When they asked Jake about it, he replied, "Just a little farther, and then you'll see for yourself."

Soon the path turned and they came to a small lake that lay glistening under the late evening sky. As they walked along the edge of the lake, the roaring became louder and louder, until suddenly they were standing by a waterfall almost two metres high. It was turning an old-fashioned waterwheel. Fascinated, the children stood and watched.

Jake was obviously pleased to be able to show them something they had never seen before. "This is where our electricity comes from," he announced. "The creek that we were following flows into this lake; here the water makes a big drop. See, the creek continues over there. We brought in a small turbine which is run by this water wheel. The turbine produces electricity, which we gather and store in the batteries at the farm."

The light was now starting to fade, so they had to hurry back. Jake led the group back to the house by another route.

The young guests were permitted to stay up a little longer. Mrs. Wentinck had fixed sandwiches for them, and although they had already had supper, they were hungry again.

“Ho-hum,” yawned Mr. Wentinck. “I think it’s high time you young folks were getting to bed. You have a long day ahead of you tomorrow.”

“Already, Uncle Klaus?” complained Carl, who liked to give his uncle a hard time. “We’re not the slightest bit sleepy yet.”

Mr. Wentinck laughed. “The girls are almost nodding off now,” he said. “And it’s time for you fellows to hit the hay too, or else we won’t be able to get you up early tomorrow morning. We get up bright and early here, you know.”

Obediently they stood up. They were actually quite tired from the long journey and the excitement. The girls went up to their little attic room, and the boys went outside to their room in the barn. Scout, of course, followed Tom, easily climbing the ladder to the loft. Upstairs stood three beds and a large basket for Scout.

“Look,” said Bert, “there’s a big door in the other wall. Is there another room behind it?”

“No,” said Carl, who had slept here before. “This used to be a regular loft. If you open that door, you drop three metres straight down.”

He slid back the bolt and pulled the handle. The heavy door swung open. Below them lay the farmyard. Jutting out above their heads was a beam with a pulley on it.

“That’s how they used to haul sacks of grain up here when this was used for storage,” Carl told the other two.

They sat looking outside for a little while. The moon had appeared and it spread a soft glow over the woods. In the distance they could still hear the faint roar of the waterfall.

Carl carefully closed the door again, and a few minutes later the three boys were lying in bed, while Scout lay curled up in his basket. It wasn’t long before they were all sleeping like roses.

CHAPTER III

The Sign of the Falcon

The next few days the five young people enjoyed themselves tremendously. There was always something new for them to experience. They explored the forests and climbed the hills. They went out into the fields with Jake and Mr. Wentinck, and helped with the farmwork. They played hide and seek around the farmyard, which provided countless places to hide. There was no time to be bored.

One day they were out again as a group following a path in the woods that was new to them. The path was full of queer twists and turns, so that finally they had little or no idea where they were.

"No matter," asserted Tom. "Scout is with us. He can always find the way back for us."

Ina pointed to the dog. "There must be people nearby," she whispered. "Look how nervous Scout is acting."

Now the others noticed it too. Their four-footed companion had his ears pricked up and was sniffing the air suspiciously, as if he had picked up the scent of strangers. Suddenly branches crackled overhead, and two men who had been hiding up in the tree dropped into the middle of the group.

Frightened, the youths jumped back a couple of steps. Scout bared his teeth threateningly.

"Halt! Customs!" barked one of the men. "Who are you? Don't you know you're not allowed to be here?"

"N-no Sir," stammered Carl, who was in the lead. "This is the first time we've been here."

"A likely story," scoffed the customs officer. "Looks to me like those smugglers have thought up a new trick: send ahead a few children to see if the coast is clear and supply them with a dog who can smell someone coming a hundred metres away. We're impounding that dog, and you children will have to come along for questioning."

This threw an awful scare into the group, especially into Tom. He stepped forward and said, "Honest, Sir, we really had no idea we were trespassing. We're guests at the Wentinck farm and we were just out for a walk in the woods. We really don't know any smugglers. Please don't take Scout away. He won't hurt anybody, and . . ."

Tom was going to say much more on behalf of Scout and themselves, but the officer interrupted him. His expression seemed less forbidden. "You're guests at the Wentincks?" he asked. "And did you say the dog's name was Scout? Hmm . . . seems to me I've heard that name before. What are your names?"

He pulled a notebook from his pocket and took down their names and addresses. Then he asked a few more questions, apparently to discover whether they were telling the truth.

Gradually both customs officers began to look a little friendlier. Finally, the man who had been doing all the talking said, "This time we'll let you and the dog go, since you're strangers in this area. But you're more than twenty metres into the border zone. If it happens again, you're in deep trouble. So, clear out, on the double, and be more careful next time."

"Thank you, Sir. We'll watch out where we're going from now on," Tom promised on behalf of the group. Then they beat a hasty retreat, relieved to get off so lightly.

The matter was still on their minds when they arrived back at the farm, where supper was waiting for them. During suppertime Mr. Wentinck gave his young guests several probing looks. They looked a bit glum, he thought. "What's the matter?" he finally asked. Then they quickly spilled what was on their minds and told him of that afternoon's adventure.

"What did the officer who did all the talking look like?" asked Wentinck.

"He was a tall, broad man with reddish hair," said Carl.

Wentinck laughed. "That was Barlinkhof," he said. "He's a tough one, all right. But he has to be, because there's so much smuggling going on of late. I know him well; he stops in here quite often."

"That's a good thing," said Tom, "because he was going to take Scout away from us at first, and it looked like we were in trouble too. But when I mentioned your name, he became a lot friendlier."

They went on talking about the incident a little longer. Jake promised his young guests that he would take them for a tour along the forbidden border zone, so that in the future they would know what was and what was not off-limits to them. The youngsters resolved that from now on they would keep their eyes wide open, because if it happened again, they might not get off so easy.

That same night, after the children had gone to bed and Mr. and Mrs. Wentinck were sitting in front of the house on a little bench, Barlinkhof came striding onto the yard. He sat down with them and began making small talk. After a while, he casually asked, "How about your young guests — have they arrived yet?"

"Yes," replied Wentinck drily, "and they're having a great time. They've even organized a smuggling ring."

The customs officer gave Wentinck a funny look, but then he began to laugh. He saw that the farmer knew what was behind the innocent question and had already heard what had happened that day.

"I really thought we had made a good catch at first," he said. "That beautiful tracking dog they had with them made me especially suspicious. We had been sitting up in that tree for quite a while, because we had reason to suspect something was going to be transported along that trail."

"Are you having more trouble with smugglers of late?" asked Mrs. Wentinck.

"Trouble isn't the word for it!" Barlinkhof exclaimed with unusual vehemence. "We're not so much concerned about the petty smuggling by people living along the border. That has always been going on and always will. But now a smuggling ring is supposed to be operating in this area, a ring with connections all over the country, and their business is estimated to run into the millions. There are indications that they're taking it across somewhere in this neighbourhood. But we can't seem to nail them. I thought I knew all the trails and tricks, but this bunch is too slick for me. And the bigwigs at headquarters are getting impatient. Sometimes I get the feeling they no longer trust those of us who are patrolling the border. Maybe they think we're in cahoots with the smugglers. But that's not true: I know these men. It's a miserable situation."

Suddenly he was silent, looking a little embarrassed that he had allowed himself to say so much.

Mrs. Wentinck hastened to pour him a cup of coffee, while Mr. Wentinck thoughtfully sucked on his pipe. Now he understood why Barlinkhof had come down so hard on those children that afternoon. He sympathized with the officer, whom he knew to be a solid, trustworthy man. Barlinkhof changed the subject. He started talking about Scout, whom he already knew from Wentinck's stories.

"A fine looking animal, that Scout," he said. "I think he'd make a great tracker. I wish I could buy him. He'd be a tremendous help on the job."

"I'm afraid you're not that fortunate," said Wentinck, laughing. "That dog isn't for sale at any price. But if you run into a situation where you could use a good tracking dog, I think Tom and Scout would be more than willing to be of service."

The next morning Wentinck told his young guests, "Barlinkhof was here last night. I'm afraid you children are in for trouble."

They looked at each other anxiously. But Carl, who knew his uncle well, spotted the ghost of a grin on the farmer's face.

"Still, there's a chance for you children. But for Scout the jig is up. Barlinkhof is going to come and pick him up in the next few days."

Tom's face fell, but Carl cried, "Don't you worry, Tom. Uncle Klaus is only pulling your leg."

Wentinck could no longer keep a straight face; laughing, he told them that Barlinkhof had really been there last night, but that he had wanted to buy Scout.

"Buy Scout!" cried Carl. "Are you kidding? Our dog isn't for sale! What did he want Scout for?"

"Well," said Wentinck, "there's a well-organized smuggling ring working in this area. When Barlinkhof stopped you yesterday, he thought you were involved with them. He'd like to have a dog like Scout to track the smugglers down. I already told him the dog wasn't for sale, but" — the farmer paused a moment — "but I told him perhaps you and Scout might be willing to give him a hand if he needed you. What do you say to that?"

"Yes! Of course!" they all shouted enthusiastically.

The rest of the morning all they could talk about was the smugglers and Scout's tracking talents.

"Wouldn't that be great if Scout could catch those bandits!" said Miriam.

But Jake, who had overheard their conversation, shook his finger at them in warning, "Careful you don't stray into the border zone again. One chance is all you get. It wouldn't be the first time innocent people who blundered into the area were picked up and tossed into jail."

"You were going to come along with us and show us how far we could go," said Ina, reminding Jake of his promise.

"I know," he said. "But I don't have any time this morning. Maybe this evening."

But the excited group of young people couldn't wait: they struck out on their own that morning, taking Scout with them. They told each other they might pick up some signs of the criminals.

The woods were refreshingly cool, ideal for a stroll. At first they kept their eyes peeled for signs of the smugglers, but when they saw nothing suspicious, they soon forgot why they had come. There were so many beautiful sights to distract them.

They spent some time watching the noisy dance of the waterfall. Although the water was shockingly cold, they took off their shoes and socks and waded upstream in the sparkling, clear water. In a clearing between the trees Miriam and Ina found many exquisite flowers and began picking them. They heard the hammering of a woodpecker, but no matter how they looked, they couldn't find the bird.

In the branches overhead was a sudden rustling. For a moment they froze in fear, because they couldn't help recalling the two customs officers who had suddenly come dropping out of a tree. But then they saw what it was. A squirrel swiftly leaped from branch to branch and from tree to tree.

"Look at him go," said Bert. "Something must have frightened him."

Just then Tom uttered a yelp of excitement. A few metres behind the squirrel followed a long, brown animal with short, stubby legs that moved over the branches with surprising speed. It had a black tail and a white spot on its throat.

"A pine marten!" cried Tom. "He's chasing the squirrel."

Both animals were fast disappearing into the woods. The children immediately gave chase, but they had trouble making enough speed through the trees and the undergrowth to keep up to the squirrel and its pursuer. Tom and Scout were in the lead. The dog, too, had been seized by the excitement of the chase and was barking noisily.

The squirrel reached the top of a tall oak tree, but its deadly pursuer was right on its heels. In utter desperation the frightened, exhausted animal launched itself at a neighbouring tree some distance from the oak. It sailed through the air, missed the branch, and crashed to the ground.

Swift as lightning, the marten flashed down the trunk of the oak tree to seize its prey. But before it reached the ground, Scout arrived. The marten spied the danger just in time and stopped, hissing furiously at the dog. Then it shot back up the tree and disappeared between the branches. The squirrel took advantage of the opportunity to disappear in another direction.

The youngsters caught up to Scout and looked around, at a loss; then they all started talking at the same time.

"I'm glad Scout saved that nice little squirrel," said Miriam. "I think that awful beast would have torn him to pieces."

"Yes," said Tom, nodding. "We spoiled his dinner all right. You should have seen how mad he was at Scout. He hissed just like a cat, but he didn't dare to challenge the dog."

Tom cast an admiring look at his dog, but Scout's attention had already been captured by something else. With his forepaws he was scratching aside the moss between the roots of the big oak. He sniffed and growled.

Carl bent forward over the dog. "There's a hollow place between the roots," he said. "Maybe Scout has found something."

But no one dared to put a hand into the hole, afraid that it might be the home of some creature. So Carl grabbed a stick and poked around in the opening. First all he felt was dirt and tree roots, but all of a sudden his stick struck something else. It sounded hollow and metallic. Now that he had made sure there were no creatures in the hole, he was no longer afraid. He dropped on his stomach and put his arm in the opening. In a moment he was pulling something out. It was an old, metal box, like a tobacco tin. "I wonder how that got there," Bert said puzzled.

"Open it," Tom urged impatiently. "Maybe there's something in it."

Carl lifted the lid. In the box was a folded piece of paper. His fingers trembled with suspense as he opened the note. They were all once again thinking of the smuggling ring.

The note was covered with letters. At least, they were marks that looked like letters. But none of the group could make sense of the marks. Tom took the note and stared at the mysterious writing. Here and there he thought he recognized a letter, but as a whole the note remained unreadable. In the middle of the strange symbols, however, he found a B followed by the number 22.

"Look," he said, "it says something about B22, but that doesn't tell us much."

Deep in thought, he folded the paper shut again, and then he noticed a figure drawn on the outside. It looked like a large bird. Everyone crowded around to examine the new discovery.

"It's a falcon," said Bert, who knew a lot about animals.

"Yes," agreed Tom, nodding. "But what does it mean?"

"Maybe it belongs to a group of boys who have developed a code and stashed the note here," suggested Carl.

"Perhaps you're right," said Tom. "It could just be part of a game. But there are very few homes around here, and I haven't seen any other children in these woods besides us. It could also have something to do with those smugglers."

"Let's take along the box and the note and show it to Barlinkhof," proposed Ina.

Carl shook his head. "If those smugglers discover that the note is gone, they'll know we're on their trail," he argued. "We should put it back and tell those customs men about it. Then they can stake out this tree to see if anybody comes to pick up the message."

They talked it over, and although they were reluctant to surrender their find, they decided to follow Carl's proposal. It made the most sense. They restored the hiding place to its original condition as well as they could. After making one more search of the area without finding anything else, they started back.

The squirrel had led them deep into the woods, and now they had some difficulty finding their way back. But finally they again found themselves in familiar surroundings. It was almost lunch time when they finally reached the farm.

CHAPTER IV

The Ancient Ruins

Over lunch the children described their adventure as the Wentincks listened with great interest.

" . . . and on the outside of the note was a big bird," said Tom.

Jake looked up in surprise. "What did it look like exactly?" he asked.

Carl, who was good at drawing, took a pencil and sheet of paper and made a sketch of the bird.

"Sure!" exclaimed Jake. "That's the coat of arms of Falconhorst. You can still see the stone sculpture on the gate of the castle ruins."

Now it was the young people's turn to look surprised. "Are there castle ruins around here? Can we see them? Why didn't you tell us before?" They were all talking at the same time.

"Oh, there are lots of things around here that you haven't seen yet," said Jake, laughing. "But, yes, there are some ancient ruins not far from here, and there is even a spooky story to go with it."

"Tell us, tell us!" demanded the whole group.

But Jake replied, "I don't have the time right now. I have to get back to work or else I won't get finished this afternoon. But maybe tonight we can take a hike to the old castle. I might even tell you the story then."

"Remember, Jake, you're not allowed inside the castle," Wentinck warned him. "And there is only one path that is safe, because I'm not sure that that minefield was ever completely cleared."

"Don't worry," said Jake. "I've been there several times since the war — once with Barlinkhof and once with De Vries, the old game warden. That *No Trespassing* sign is really only for outsiders who don't know about the dangers."

But Jake's father insisted that they shouldn't go into the ruins. "You can see them well enough from the outside," he said. "Later we can ask Barlinkhof to take you inside for a closer look."

Jake wasn't entirely happy with the arrangement, but his father's word was law to him. The others were in a dither to get going, but they had to wait. It was just as well, for the weather was oppressively hot that afternoon. The sun burned bright in a cloudless sky.

The five young guests sought the shade of a big tree in front of the house and sat down in the grass to read and talk. It was so hot, however, that they almost fell asleep.

"Whew!" said Tom after awhile, yawning. "Am I ever sleepy! It's too warm to read."

Most of the others were already stretched out in the grass. The whole group might have dozed off if Scout, lying beside Tom with his head on his forepaws hadn't suddenly pricked up his ears and begun growling softly.

"Somebody's coming. Look at Scout," said Ina.

The next moment they heard violin music. Around the corner of the farmhouse came an old man. He had a brown leathery face, dark eyes and was quite short. The children stared at the unexpected arrival in surprise.

"He must be a gypsy," whispered Carl. "A lot of them can really play the fiddle."

This man played extremely well. The bow darted over the violin strings while the children listened breathlessly. The man coaxed a mesmerizing melody from his instrument. It was strange and haunting; it made you feel almost sad, it was so beautiful. Suddenly he stopped playing. The violin uttered one last wailing note and then fell silent.

Slowly, as if he were gliding, the strange man came closer. His eyes, black as coals, were fixed on Scout. A growl rose from deep in Scout's throat and his hair bristled, but the old gypsy didn't seem at all afraid. He said something to the dog in a strange, melodious language which none of the young people understood. Scout continued to be wary of the man, but he also seemed to have a certain respect for him, because he didn't start barking and made no attempt to attack him.

The gypsy turned to Tom, and with a heavy accent, he said, "Beautiful dog. Very beautiful. He is a good tracker, yes?"

Tom had overcome his initial bashfulness, and proudly he answered, "There isn't a better tracker in the whole country. He has proven himself several times already."

The old man again gave Scout a penetrating look. "You give me that dog," he said suddenly. "I take good care of him. Then I tell you future."

"I wouldn't part with Scout for anything," Tom said coldly, "and . . . and," he continued hesitantly, "you don't know the future. Only God knows that." He blushed as he said it. It sounded so funny to be saying it to a stranger. But it was true.

The gypsy was about to reply, but at that moment Jake came driving onto the yard as he returned from the fields with the wagon. He reined in the horse, jumped down and walked toward the group.

"Hi Wasil," he said. "Nice to see you again. We love your music. But you're not bothering these children with any of your palm-reading and other mumbo-jumbo are you? Because we don't believe in that kind of stuff."

"He was going to tell us the future if we would give him Scout," said Carl.

Meanwhile, the old gypsy had walked over to the horse, which stood waiting patiently in front of the wagon. He patted the horse on the neck and studied him like an expert judge of horseflesh.

"Wasil used to be a horse dealer," Jake told them. "He knows an awful lot about horses, although I'm not sure I'd buy one from him. He knows too many tricks."

Mrs. Wentinck came outside and called the children in for tea. Wasil followed them into the house. While Mrs. Wentinck and Hanna served tea and buttermilk to the thirsty youngsters, the gypsy again tucked his violin under his chin and played another melody. When it was finished, he, too, had a cup of tea and several sandwiches, which he devoured hungrily. Mrs. Wentinck also wrapped a few sandwiches for him to take along on his travels.

"Doesn't the heat bother you, Wasil?" asked Jake.

The old man grinned. "I should complain about such beautiful weather? It's cold weather I don't like. We gypsies, we love the sun. I go. Thank you very much."

The young people watched the strange figure go. He left the yard and disappeared into the woods.

"What a strange man!" said Ina. "But he could sure play."

"Wasil has been living around here for years," Jake told them. "He disappeared during the German occupation. We thought the

Germans had picked him up, but apparently he had only moved to another part of the country. He came back here soon after we were liberated. He lives all by himself in a small trailer close to town. They say he comes from somewhere in Eastern Europe and that he used to be rich. But there doesn't seem to be much left of his wealth, because he earns his living travelling around playing his violin."

"I thought he was kind of eerie," said Miriam. "Does he steal children?"

"He has enough trouble feeding himself," said Jake, laughing. "People say that gypsies steal, but Wasil has never given anybody any trouble."

Jake went back to work and the group of young people went on talking. They were eagerly looking forward to that evening and the hike to the old castle.

After supper it was still oppressively hot. But when Jake asked them if they still felt like going out, the young guests shouted with one voice, "Yes, of course!"

"Okay," said Jake, "then let's get started."

Meanwhile, Mr. Wentinck had been studying the sky. "I don't like the looks of it," he said. "We could be in for quite a thunderstorm tonight. Keep an eye on the weather, Jake. If the sky gets any darker, you'd better head straight back."

Jake promised his father they would be careful, and the group set off, filled with high expectations. Once they got into the woods, the heat wasn't quite as bad, although the air still hung heavy about them.

The five youngsters had begun to think they knew the woods quite well already. But they saw that Jake was far more at home in the woods than they. He took them down numerous new paths, showed them unusual flowers, pointed out the lair of a badger — a shy and seldom seen denizen of the woods — and seemed to have an inexhaustible supply of woodlore. The youngsters were enjoying the hike tremendously. Their attention was continually caught by something new. As a result, they didn't notice the sky becoming darker and darker. Under the dense canopy of trees, very little of the sky was visible. And they didn't notice the light beginning to fade in the woods.

"We've made quite a detour," said Jake at last. "I guess it's time we were heading for the castle, because we have a long hike back."

They turned down new paths through a dense, gloomy pine forest, until suddenly they emerged at the edge of an immense heath, which, said Jake, extended all the way into Germany. In the middle of the field, a few hundred metres from where they were standing, rose the sombre stone remains of the old castle. Still standing was part of the ancient gate and parts of the walls. A small section of the castle seemed still to be in fairly good shape. Rising defiantly erect out of the ruins was one round, corner tower. At its base were other parts that were still intact too.

"That's Falconhorst," said Jake. "You can't see it too well from this distance, but they're fascinating ruins. Too bad my father ordered us to stay away from it. I know the path very well, and there's really no danger."

The children stood looking quietly. The ancient ruins with the dark, imposing tower made a spooky impression on them.

Jake had meanwhile turned an anxious eye to the sky. "We haven't been paying attention to the weather," he said. "I forgot my father's warning. It looks like we're in for a whopper of a thunderstorm."

No sooner were the words out of his mouth than a blinding bolt of lightning cleft the sky, followed a few seconds later by a reverberating clap of thunder.

It frightened the youngsters. Especially the two girls cast anxious looks at Jake. But he didn't seem to know what to do. "There are no homes around here where we can hide from the rain," he said. "And it will start any minute. We could find cover under some big trees, but that' s dangerous during a thunderstorm."

Another bright bolt of lightning blazed across the sky. The sky was black with threatening clouds, which were swiftly moving toward the group of young people. The girls jumped back fearfully at the blinding light and the booming rumble that followed. The boys, too, stirred uneasily.

Jake saw that he had to take the lead. Resolutely he turned to the others. "There's only one thing we can do," he said. "The only shelter around here is in those ruins. My father didn't know we were going to be caught in this. He'd have to agree that the castle is the safest place for us to be. Come on, let's go."

"Won't that tower attract lightning just as much as a tree?" asked Tom.

"Just before the war a lightning rod was put on top of the tower because it had been hit a couple of times," explained Jake. "They were going to repair the castle a little so it wouldn't deteriorate any further. But nothing came of it because of the war. If that lightning rod is still working, we should be pretty safe in the tower."

As he talked they were hurrying along the outskirts of the heath to the place where the path to the castle began.

"Stay right behind me," said Jake, "then you'll be safe."

The others did as he said. Tom signalled Scout to stay close beside him to keep him from running into the dangerous mine field. The path was little more than a faint trail. Here and there the heath had grown over it. Because it took a couple of turns, Jake had to be very careful not to lose his way.

When they were halfway down the path, the sky was again set ablaze with lightning, and before the thunder drowned all other sounds out, they heard the cracking of a tree. Not far behind them a tree had been struck. The youngsters froze in fright. Ina started crying. Raindrops began to fall.

"Quick!" said Jake. "We've got to hurry. It will be pouring in another minute. In the tower we'll be dry and safe."

The last part of the trail was wider and easier to follow. Jake broke into a trot and the others followed him as fast as they could. The rain was now beginning in earnest and the sky had grown even darker.

The crumbling castle gate towered before them. Long ago the castle had been surrounded by a moat spanned by a drawbridge, but the moat was overgrown and the bridge had been replaced by an earthen dam. As they crossed the dam, by the light of another lightning flash, they saw the stone figure of a large falcon above the gate. It looked just like the bird in the mysterious note. They had no time for sightseeing, however. In the pouring rain they hurried across the inner court of the castle, stumbling occasionally on the rough ground. Through a break in one of the walls, they came into a large hall, but the roof was gone.

Moving as fast as he could, Jake led them into a long hallway. A little later they were standing in a small room that already provided them some protection from the rain. It was completely dark here, but Jake seemed to know his way around. He went to one of the walls, groped around a moment, and then found a heavy latch. Soon a door was squeaking open. "Come on. We'll be fine in here," Jake said, inviting the others in. They followed somewhat hesitantly. It was very dark and spooky here.

They were now standing in a circular room, sheltered from the rain and wind. In the wall were two narrow, arched windows that had at one time apparently held bars and glass, but which were now merely tall holes in the massive stone walls. They let very little light into the room. After their eyes got used to the darkness, however, the young people could see more clearly. Moreover, the lightning flashes, which were now following closely on top of one another, repeatedly lit up the interior. The round room was almost completely empty, except for two stone benches along the wall. There was also a stone stairway that led upward to other stories.

"We're in the tall corner tower that we saw from far away," said Jake. "This is the best preserved part of the castle. Let's sit down on those benches over there."

They sat down close together, Scout lying down on the floor beside Tom. The German shepherd seemed uneasy. He kept sniffing the air and sometimes he uttered a low growl.

"I wonder what's bothering Scout," said Tom. "He's acting so strange."

"Oh, he smells the rats, of course," said Jake. "I'm sure it's crawling with rats in here, and he has caught their scent, no doubt."

"Gross! Rats?" shuddered Ina. "Those are the most gruesome creatures! I saw one once: it had a long skinny tail. I hope they don't come near us."

“Don’t worry,” said Jake. “Those rats aren’t stupid. They’ve smelled the dog too, and they won’t show themselves with him around.”

The group of young adventurers sat back to wait out the thunderstorm, but the rain did not let up and the thunder rumbled almost continuously. Gradually, however, it began to grow lighter.

Jake was standing on the other bench, which was right underneath one of the windows, and was looking outside. “It will be at least another fifteen minutes before we can leave,” he said. “This is a good time to tell you the story I promised to tell you about this castle.”

The five youngsters didn’t have to be asked twice. Eagerly they gathered around Jake, making themselves comfortable as he began his story.

CHAPTER V

The Mystery of Falconhorst

"Falconhorst Castle was built long ago during the Middle Ages by a nobleman who owned all the land and villages in this entire area. Not much is known about the man. It was a chaotic time. The nobles, who were supposed to protect the people, were instead their worst enemy. The first Lord Falconhorst was also supposed to have been one of these pillaging nobles. So when he built the castle, he made it as strong as possible to protect himself from the vengeance of his enemies.

"Later in the sixteenth century an old nobleman called Ewald van Falconhorst lived in the castle. He was a good man who looked after his poor serfs like a father. Ewald had two children: a son called Baldwin and a daughter called Ada. They were happy together, although Ewald continued to grieve for his wife who had died giving birth to Ada. It was the time of the Reformation. In Falconhorst, too, the writings of Luther and Calvin were read. Lord Ewald gradually became more and more convinced that the Roman Catholic Church had strayed far from God's Word. He obtained a Bible and he and his children began to read it.

"Sometimes pedlars came to the castle gate. They were always well-received and were admitted by Lord Ewald himself, for in those days many pedlars also carried, concealed among their wares, books and pamphlets which defended the Reformation teachings and exposed the Roman Catholic Church as a false church. Lord Ewald also discussed the Bible with the people living in the castle and with his serfs.

"In a village nearby there lived a priest who was also sympathetic to the 'new teachings.' He and his parishioners stripped all the statues from the church and he began to preach from the Bible.

"But the priest in the next village was of a different mind. He, too, felt that many things happening in the church were wrong, but he told his people not to leave the Roman Catholic Church. The

Pope and other leaders of the church would soon correct the abuses, he said. Most of the people listened to him. That's why over three hundred years later most of the people in the other village are still Roman Catholic while in our village almost everyone is Protestant."

"And what happened at the castle?" asked Bert.

"Well," said Jake. "Young Baldwin went to Geneva, where John Calvin had founded a theological university, and he became a student there. He wrote many enthusiastic letters to his aging father and sister back at Falconhorst.

"The father and daughter led quite lonely lives in the castle. But one day they got an unexpected visitor. A knight on a spirited horse came dashing up to the gate. They knew him well. His name was Black Bertram, the lord of a large territory that lay about two hours to the south. Lord Ewald was very surprised to see Black Bertram. The knight had a bad reputation. He led a loose life with his cronies and oppressed his peasants. When he was with his friends, he liked to make fun of the church and the clergy, but he would have nothing to do with the Reformation. He liked the Reformed even less.

"Lord Ewald received him very politely. He asked him to sit down in a large chair and the dutiful Ada poured him a cup of wine. Bertram had dark, piercing eyes and a pale face that was marred by a long scar he had picked up in a duel. He got his name from his jet black hair.

"When Ada left the room, Ewald quickly learned the reason for Bertram's visit. The knight, who was still unmarried, had come to ask the Lord of Falconhorst for the hand of his daughter. It shocked the old man tremendously, for the wild and godless Bertram was the last person he wanted as a husband for his daughter. Besides, the man was almost twenty years older than the young girl.

"The host replied quite honestly that the offer came as a complete surprise to him and that he would first have to ask his daughter if she wished to become Sir Bertram's wife. Ada was called back into the room. When her father told her of the knight's offer, the slender young girl leaned against her father's chair, pale and trembling. She hesitated a moment and then she answered with strong resolution, 'I cannot marry Sir Bertram. I don't love him and I'm afraid he does not love God, and it is my highest desire to serve Him.' Then she turned and left the room.

"When she closed the door behind her, the black-haired knight cursed angrily. Then he turned to his host and demanded that he force his daughter to marry him. But Lord Ewald turned this down cold and told Bertram he agreed with his daughter's decision.

"Foaming at the mouth with fury, Black Bertram finally stormed out of the castle, shouting terrible threats. And he swore that he would avenge himself for the way this old heretic and his daughter had insulted him.

"Lord Ewald and his daughter soon put the matter out of their minds. There were so many other things demanding their attention. For it was a confusing time in this part of Europe, and many strange things were happening. People poured out of the cities to listen to the outdoor preachers and stormed back into the cities to strip the churches of their images. Finally, King Philip of Spain sent the Duke of Alva to the Netherlands to restore order. The Prince of Orange, whom many looked to for help, had fled to Germany, where he was trying to raise money to build an army. Lord Ewald, too, sent him a large sum.

"Baldwin wrote from Geneva that he had finished his studies but wasn't coming home. He was going to join the Prince of Orange to help liberate the Dutch from King Philip's tyranny.

"At Falconhorst and in the nearby village everything remained relatively peaceful. The church was controlled by people sympathetic to the Reformation, and the priest, who was now the preacher, was faithfully preaching sound doctrine.

"Then came the news that two brothers of the Prince of Orange, Lodewyk and Adolf of Nassau invaded the north with a large army and had defeated the Spanish at Heiligerlee. It was the first victory for the freedom fighters, but it cost Count Adolf his life.[1] A short time later, a secret messenger brought Ewald a letter from Baldwin, who was with Lodewyk's army. The young nobleman said he was very hopeful and expected to be home soon. He thought it wouldn't be long before the whole country was liberated and everyone would be free to worship God according to His Word.

---

[1] See: *Dispelling the Tyranny* by Piet Prins

"But he was wrong. Alva met Lodewyk's troops with a well-drilled army and overwhelmed them. Lord Ewald and Ada were extremely worried about Baldwin. For weeks there was no news. But finally one of Baldwin's companions in arms brought them the sad news that the young man had given his life for the cause.

"Many tears were shed for him at Falconhorst. But the nobleman and his daughter found comfort in God's Word. They knew that Baldwin had loved Jesus and that he was better off now than he had ever been on earth.

"It was a fearful time. The merciless Alva ruled supreme and all Dutch Protestants were ruthlessly persecuted. The church in the village here was taken out of protestant hands and the images put back. A Roman Catholic priest took the place of the preacher, who had fled to Germany.

"Then Black Bertram saw his chance to avenge himself. One day a letter with a large seal on the outside was delivered to the castle of Falconhorst. It was from a Spanish inquisitor, and it ordered Lord Ewald and his daughter to come and answer to charges of heresy.

"But the old nobleman knew what was in store for them if they obeyed the order. Perhaps if he had been alone he would have gone, but because Ada's life was also in danger, he refused. He wrote back pointing out that, according to the laws of the land, the inquisitor had no right to summon them. And he declared that he and his daughter were not heretics or schismatics, but people struggling to live by the Word of God.

"Lord Ewald hoped that they would be left in peace. This was a strong castle with many faithful men to defend it. Besides, it lay rather isolated on the Eastern border of the country. Perhaps the inquisition would make no attempt to seize him.

"With the help of his serfs, he strengthened the castle as well as he could. They deepened the moat, checked all the walls, doors, and windows, and made ready to defend themselves.

"First nothing happened. But a few weeks later another letter arrived from the inquisitor. It announced that, because they had refused to appear before the inquisition, they were declared fair game to anyone who wished to kill them and seize their property. Lord Ewald was terribly shocked, but he knew he was safe in God's hands, and he also knew he could count on the loyalty of his serfs, most of whom had also adopted the Reformed faith.

"A short time later, however, he heard that Black Bertram was hiring large numbers of mercenaries and buying canons. Before the Lord of Falconhorst could take further measures to defend himself, the army of ruffians was already at his gate. Bertram came in such force that Ewald's serfs saw they didn't have a chance, so they fled, for Bertram killed all those he captured and burned their homes to the ground. He demanded the castle's surrender, promising to spare Lord Ewald if he handed over his daughter and all his possessions.

"The old nobleman, of course, rejected the offer, and his men, too, were determined to defend their liege lord and his daughter to the death. With his canons Black Bertram eventually managed to breach the castle walls. Branches were stacked in the moat to form a bridge, and the bloodthirsty mob stormed the castle.

"But the defenders didn't yield a step; they fought courageously. Many of the attackers fell before them, but their numbers were too great. Finally Lord Ewald, who was fighting at the head of his men, was forced to give the signal to retreat into hallways of the castle. They would continue their resistance from there. But the enemy was so close on the heels of the retreating defenders that they had no chance to establish another line of defence. They were simply forced back farther and farther until they were fighting in the hallway leading to this corner tower.

"Here Black Bertram, brandishing a huge broadsword, finally came face to face with his enemy. There was a wicked grin on his face and an evil glint in his eyes. But, although he was old, Lord Ewald gave a good account of himself. He had not lost his martial skills. In fact, he even managed to wound his opponent in the side. But thereupon one of Bertram's men hurled a block of wood at his feet, causing him to stumble. With a shout of triumph Black Bertram cut down the old man, giving him a fatal wound.

"To keep their lord from falling into enemy hands Ewald's men made a furious sally forward, forcing the attackers to retreat momentarily. The door of the corner tower burst open and Ada came running out. She had heard that her father had been mortally wounded and was blind to all danger. She knelt beside her wounded

father and took his head in her arms so that his blood stained her clothes.

"The dying man gave her a last look filled with love and whispered, 'You know what you promised me, Ada. Now is the time. It's too late for me. I am going to heaven to join your brother. Always remain true to God's Word.' Then, in the arms of his daughter, he expelled his last breath.

"Meanwhile Bertram's men attacked with renewed strength. They had the defenders with their backs to the wall. But the remainder of Lord Ewald's men just succeeded in pulling the weeping Ada into the corner tower with them, closing the door behind them and barring it.

"Black Bertram was almost beside himself. It wouldn't be long and Ada would be in his hands. When he couldn't force the door open, he ordered his men to fetch a big beam. Using this as a battering ram, they finally knocked down the door.

"The victorious attackers finally stormed into the defender's last stronghold. Bertram was the first through the door. He was carrying a torch because the fighting had raged all day and darkness had already set in. That was in this very room. He looked around."

Jake paused a moment. The others sat around him listening with bated breath and glowing eyes. They had forgotten the thunderstorm and didn't even notice that it had become lighter outside.

"What then?" asked Tom, because Jake was purposely stretching out the pause.

"Well," Jake replied slowly, lowering his voice, "Black Bertram and his soldiers entered this room with their torches, and to their surprise, they saw that it was empty."

"Empty?" the children echoed in disbelief.

"Yes, empty," repeated Jake. "All the defenders were gone. Ada and the last of Lord Ewald's men had disappeared.

"Bertram cursed and ranted. He ran up the stone stairway to the second story. He even climbed up into the peak of the tower, but there wasn't a trace of the girl or the men. Then he exploded in a fit of fury. He screamed at the soldiers that they had let the girl escape, even though he knew that this was impossible. He picked a quarrel with the commander of the mercenaries and raised such a row that the man left in a huff, taking his men with him.

"But Black Bertram and some of his men stayed in the castle. He spent the entire night looking for traces of the fugitives. The next day, too, he refused to leave the castle. He couldn't accept the fact that Ada had still escaped him in the end. After his men finally took him back to his own castle, almost dragging him, he lost himself in wild drinking parties. When his cronies were gone and his hangover had worn off, however, he often sat for days mutely staring ahead of him. Some say he finally lost his sanity as divine punishment for what he had done."

"And what happened to Ada? How did she escape, and where did she go?" asked Miriam.

Jake spread his hands and shrugged his shoulders.

"The story I told you is a very old one, of course," he said, "and it has never been written down. It is told by the villagers around here and passed from father to child to grandchild. No one knows if everything happened exactly as the story says it did. But a lot of people, including some historians, believe that the main facts are true. Apparently Ada did escape from the castle somehow, although no one has ever found out how she could have done so. She is said to have lived in Emden and later in London, where a Dutch refugee congregation existed for many years. There she is supposed to have married an English nobleman who also professed the Reformed faith. They say that she had a very happy marriage."

CHAPTER VI

The Face in the Tower

The young people were sorry that Jake's story had come to an end. They asked numerous questions, but Jake could give them no further details of the mysterious legend. All he knew was that the castle had later been rebuilt but had finally been allowed to fall into disrepair. It had been an uninhabited ruin for hundreds of years now.

"Do you think maybe that metal box we found under the tree has something to do with the story?" Carl asked hesitantly. "The note had a falcon on it just like the one over the gate of the castle. Maybe it had been lying there between those roots for hundreds of years."

Jake laughed. "I don't think so," he said. "The box would have long since rusted through and the note turned into dust. And you boys said they both looked clean and new. Still, it does seem strange. Tell me again: how did you stumble on the box and what did the note say?"

With the help of the others, Tom described in detail what they had done that afternoon. And they also tried to recall everything that had been written on the note. But they hadn't been able to decipher anything except the letter B followed by the number 22.

Jake shrugged his shoulders. "I haven't the foggiest idea what it could mean," he said. "But tomorrow we'll tell the customs men about it. If they think the tree is used as a message drop by the smugglers, maybe they'll post a couple of men to watch the tree and see if anyone comes to pick up the note."

The rest of the group agreed this was a good plan. Meanwhile, Jake had jumped up on the stone bench standing under the tower window. He looked outside and said, "The thunderstorm is past, although I can still see lightning in the distance. The rain has also stopped. We've stayed here too long, because the sun is already beginning to set. We'd better get moving."

They all stood up. The young people took one more close look around the room, which was slightly lighter now than when they had first entered. This was where the story had happened, according to Jake. It was spooky, but also very fascinating.

They walked through the ruined halls and rooms of the ancient castle, across the courtyard and out through the gate. The large stone falcon was still there and it seemed to stare after them mockingly as they walked away.

Scout seemed to be happy to be leaving the castle. He had been constantly on edge in the tower room, but now he exuberantly went springing ahead of Tom, so that Tom had to call him to heel because he was afraid the dog would dash out into the minefield.

With Jake in the lead, they carefully followed the path until they reached the edge of the woods. There they stopped as if by a prearranged signal to take one last look at the castle. The ancient, stone tower rose dark and gloomy against the evening sky.

Suddenly a bolt of lightning shattered the sky. Miriam screamed and the boys jumped in sudden fright.

They had all seen it. The bright flash of the lightning bolt had lit up the dark tower for just a fraction of a second. The window opening through which Jake had looked out several times had been clearly visible to them. And in the window opening during that fraction of a second they had seen a pale face framed by a wild mass of black hair.

In the twilight after the bright bolt of lightning, they stood frozen to the spot for a moment. Another sheet of lightning lit the sky, less brilliantly this time. They stared at the window, but the face had disappeared. Finally they recovered their voices.

"What . . . what an awful face!" stammered Tom.

"Black Bertram!" whispered Miriam, who had turned deathly pale.

They were all unsettled. But Jake was the first one to recover his wits. "That can't be," he said firmly. "Black Bertram has been dead for hundreds of years."

"Then what was it?" Bert asked fearfully. "Do you think it was his . . ."

Jake shook his head impatiently. “I wish I hadn’t told you children that story,” he said. “Not if you’re going to start babbling about ghosts. It was probably just our imagination. I didn’t see anything at the second flash.”

“It wasn’t our imagination,” Carl said with conviction. “I clearly saw the face of a wild-looking man. I don’t believe in ghosts, but I’m pretty sure that was how Black Bertram looked.”

Jake thought they had talked long enough. The thunderstorm was completely over now and it was fast growing dark. They hurried through the darkening woods toward the farm. It was deliciously cool out, and the air, flooded with fragrances, was refreshing as it can be only after a thundershower. But the young explorers were not happy. They walked close together as if seeking protection against unseen dangers. And the two young girls especially flinched at every sound. Jake, who was walking in front, was lost deep in thought. Now and then he shook his head and clenched his hands. He was sorry their outing had taken such a turn. If only he had paid more attention on the way up, they wouldn’t have been caught in the thunderstorm, and nothing would have happened. He could sense how frightened the others were. And it was his fault.

Only Scout seemed to be without a care in the world. His sharp canine eyes weren’t bothered by the darkness, and he playfully chased anything that moved in the bushes.

When they finally spotted the lights of the farmhouse, they heaved a sigh of relief. In a few minutes they were walking onto the yard. Mr. Wentinck was standing at the door looking out for them. His face brightened visibly when he saw that they were all unharmed; nevertheless, there was a strong note of disappointment in his voice when he said to Jake, “I thought I could safely leave our guests in your hands, but it seems I was wrong.”

Jake flushed deeply and didn’t know what to say. The young people filed into the living room, where Mrs. Wentinck and Hanna were sitting. Then Jake told his parents what had happened.

He admitted that he hadn’t paid enough attention to the sky, so that they had been caught unawares by the thunderstorm and had been forced to seek shelter in the ruins.

Now that they were sitting in the shelter and security of the living room in the warm glow of the lamp, the five youngsters were a little embarrassed by their fearfulness. They were chagrined that Jake was being blamed for what had happened and assured Mr. Wentinck that Jake had taken good care of them, and that they had thoroughly enjoyed themselves.

"When we were in the tower, Jake told us a wonderful story about Ada and Black Bertram," said Ina.

"I see," the farmer said drily. "So Jake thought that was a good time and place to tell you that grisly old tale, did he?"

Jake blushed again. "All right, maybe I didn't behave very brightly," he admitted. "But we did see something strange."

He told them about the weird face they had seen in the window for one fraction of a second. Wentinck and his wife listened very attentively. They didn't laugh at Jake and the children, because they could see that the whole group had been deeply unsettled by the incident.

Jake's father thought for a moment. "I think you children were the victims of your own imaginations," he concluded. "That happens sometimes. You became so involved in the story of Black Bertram that you mistook a weird shadow for his face. Long ago there used to be a lot of superstitious people in this area who believed that the ruins were haunted."

"You mean it could have been Black . . ." began Ina.

"No," Mr. Wentinck said very seriously, "don't believe any of it. The Bible says that the dead go directly to their eternal destination: the believer to Christ Jesus and the unbeliever to the outer darkness. The church has always warned those who call upon the deceased, and who resort to or confide in sorcery, fortune-telling, charms, or other forms of superstition, not to come to the Lord's Supper. And those who continue in such sins can have no part in the kingdom of Christ."

Mr. Wentinck spoke so seriously the young people fell silent for a while.

"But there was something strange about that face in the tower," said Jake. "It really looked like a real face."

"That could be too. Maybe some hobo was using the castle as a place to sleep," said Wentinck. "Maybe when he heard you children coming, he hid in the hall or one of the other rooms, and then when you left he went to the window to watch you go."

"Remember how uneasy Scout was when we were in the tower?" Tom reminded the others. "He kept growling and sniffing about."

The farmer stood up and stretched. "It's high time for everybody to be off to bed," he said, as he reached for the Bible. "When you get the chance, you should tell the customs officers about the mysterious letter you found and also about that face in the tower. Perhaps they'll investigate and see what's going on."

After Bible-reading and prayers the girls went to their room upstairs and the boys and Scout to their room in the loft. And it wasn't long before they were all in a deep and restful sleep.

CHAPTER VII

The Padlocked Shed

The young guests were awakened by a brilliant sunrise. The heat of the previous day had disappeared and the rain made the trees and flowers look bright and fresh.

There was a lot of work to be done on the farm today. The five guests helped with numerous odd jobs that morning. After dinner they were ready to go back to work again, but Mr. Wentinck wouldn't hear of it. "You're here for a vacation," he declared, "not to spend the whole day working. Go on, we'll get along without you. There are still plenty of things around here you haven't seen."

Out of a drawer he dug a map that showed all the hiking trails in the area, and he pointed to a spot with his finger. "This is a nice area. It isn't all covered with woods: there are beautiful hills and meadows and places where you can see for long distances. I'm sorry I can't let Jake go with you, but I'm sure you can find it by yourselves. Take the map along and make sure you're back by suppertime."

They were all in the mood for a long hike. Hanna wrapped something for them to eat on the way, and off they marched in high spirits, with Scout trotting beside them. They were in no hurry. There were so many new and beautiful things to see, they kept stopping.

The woods gradually gave way to parkland — fields and meadows broken by stretches of forest. Above the rolling landscape stretched a blue sky with a few fluffy white clouds drifting overhead. Here and there a picturesque farm rose out of the vast fields, and a few people could be seen working the land.

By now the sun was much hotter than it had been in the morning, but occasionally it was screened by a big cloud, and the oppressive heat of yesterday did not return. The weather was ideal for hiking, and the young people were enjoying themselves thoroughly. Scout was in the best mood of all. He dashed and jumped about, barking playfully at every butterfly that flitted by and roughhousing with his five companions.

After a few hours they came to a small river, that wound through the fields. Here they rested awhile. Taking their time, they ate the bun and apple that Hanna had packed for each of them.

It was taking too long as far as Scout was concerned. First he tried to get Tom to chase him, and then he tried to start a wrestling match with each of the others. But all of them were feeling the effect of the long walk in their legs and were more than content to sit in the shadow of the trees and watch the water flow by. Scout grew impatient and went exploring the immediate area by himself. He flushed several birds out of the undergrowth and ran back and forth across the meadow beside the river.

His antics caused a small herd of sheep grazing in the meadow to break into a frightened run. Glad to have some playmates at last, Scout bounded after them. The sheep panicked and began running faster and faster. The dog, who had no evil intent whatsoever, thought it a wonderful game. Barking he followed the stampeding herd.

Tom, who had noticed nothing at first, now jumped to his feet. "Scout, come back here!" he shouted. But the dog was too far away and didn't hear him. A second later the sheep and the dog disappeared over a ridge.

"We have to go after him," Tom said anxiously. "Scout is only playing but he's liable to drive those sheep into a tizzy."

They all quickly scrambled to their feet and hurried across the pasture in the direction where Scout had disappeared. When they reached the crest of the ridge five minutes later, to their relief they saw the sheep grazing peacefully below. But where was Scout? No matter where they looked, he was nowhere to be seen.

"I don't understand it," muttered Tom. "Scout never runs very far off. He has to be somewhere around here."

Bert pointed to an old farm not too far off. "Maybe he's wandering around over there somewhere. In any case we might find someone around there who has seen him."

They walked toward the farm, constantly keeping an eye out for their vanished companion. Tom was very uneasy; a suspicion was growing in him that he preferred not to express.

They approached the farm from the rear. There was no one to be seen on the large yard. A flock of chickens was scratching around near the house, and in a nearby ditch a few ducks were swimming.

Tom stopped just before he reached the yard. "Scout! Here, Scout!" he called as loud as he could.

To everyone's relief, the call was immediately answered by a loud barking that they recognized at once. Scout was somewhere nearby, but he still didn't show himself. Again Tom called his name, and again Scout responded.

Now they heard where the barking was coming from: from a small shack in the backyard. They quickly ran toward it. It was a solidly built shack and the door was padlocked. Tom peered through a small window. It was dark inside, but after a few seconds he could make out the German shepherd. For the rest, the shed was empty. When he noticed his master, Scout jumped anxiously against the door, barking wildly.

"Easy, Boy! We'll have you out of there in a minute," Tom said soothingly. He went back to the door and tried the padlock, but it was securely locked. The others stood behind him in a small semi-circle.

"What's going on here?" a harsh voice demanded right behind them. The five young people jumped in fright. They looked behind them and saw a broad-shouldered giant glaring down at them.

"We . . . uh . . . my dog is locked in the shed and I was trying to get him out," Tom replied uncertainly.

"So! Is that sheep killer yours? That's going to cost you, young fella! And that dog is staying in there. He's going to be shot."

"Scout is no sheep killer! He was only playing!" Tom cried in alarm.

The farmer's expression grew even harder. "Listen," he said. "Ten days ago eight of my sheep were killed and two of my neighbours's. They were killed by a dog. And some of my farm-hands have seen a strange German shepherd roaming around here. I've been looking for the killer ever since. Finally I've caught him."

"That wasn't Scout! He wouldn't do such a thing! Ten days ago we weren't even here yet and neither was our dog!" Now the children were all talking at the same time trying to convince the farmer.

But he was unmoved. “I don’t believe it,” he said. “That dog stays in there. I saw him chasing the sheep with my own eyes.”

“But he didn’t attack any of them, did he?”

“No, those killer dogs only attack at night. I suckered the beast into that shed, and that’s where he’s going to stay until the police come and pick him up to destroy him. And someone’s going to have to pay for those sheep. Tell me, what are you children doing here and where do you live?”

Tom gave the man his name and address. The farmer took it down in a small notebook. “Hm, tourists of course. Wreck things around here and vanish without a trace! Well, this time you won’t get away with it.”

“We’re not tourists and we didn’t wreck anything!” Carl insisted. “We’re here visiting my Uncle Claus Wentinck, and we only arrived this past week with Scout. If your sheep were killed ten days ago, then this dog had nothing to do with it.”

For the first time, the farmer began to look a little doubtful. He scratched the back of his head thoughtfully.

“At the Wentincks, eh? A good man, Wentinck. And you only arrived this week?” He turned that over in his mind for a while. Then his expression became just as stubborn as before.

“I don’t know whether to believe you. As long as I’m not sure, that dog stays locked up. I don’t want anymore sheep killed. The police will check out your story.”

All their further entreaties did no good. Finally Ina and Miriam started to cry and then the farmer chased them all off the yard with a stream of angry words. They heard Scout barking helplessly but didn’t know what to do.

Forlornly they gathered on the dirt road that ran past the farm. They did not want to leave their four-footed companion behind. But what could they do to free him? Ina and Miriam, who had dried their tears, came up with all kinds of fantastic schemes to free him by trickery and force if need be. But Tom shook his head emphatically. “Forget it. We’d have to wait until after dark, and even then . . . No, we have to do something else. That farmer said he was going to the police. We’ll be one step ahead of him and report what happened before he does. After all, he stole our dog and refuses to give him back. All the Wentincks can testify that Scout wasn't here ten days ago. If we hurry, maybe we can get him back before tonight."

They all nodded their agreement. Tom's way was smart and practical. That was what they would do.

"Let's first go back to my uncle's house," suggested Carl. "And then to the police. We made a big circle during our hike. Now we have to find the shortest route back. I think if we go this way . . ." He pointed to a trail that led across the fields. Carl was the only one who had been here before and who knew the area a little, so the others immediately acknowledged his leadership.

The trail led them over a low hill. When they had crossed the top of the hill and the farm had dropped out of sight behind them, they felt a sense of relief. At least now that angry farmer couldn't see them anymore.

They descended into a wide, deep valley with cows grazing on the slopes. The trail crossed a dirt road full of deep ruts. They slackened their walking speed a little, for they had already come a long way and still had almost two hours to go.

They were heading straight for a drainage ditch. The trail crossed the ditch over an earthen dam, which was blocked by a gate. The gate had been tied shut with a thick rope. Rather than trying to loosen the rope, they nimbly climbed over the gate.

Suddenly their attention was caught by a mournful bleating. A little farther down the ditch a calf was trapped in the water up to his neck.

"Oh, that poor thing!" cried Miriam. "We've got to do something." She trotted toward it, followed by the others

The young animal was in bad trouble. The ditch was quite deep here and contained a lot of water. Apparently the calf, already a hefty, good-sized animal, had tried to take a drink and had slid down the steep, slippery bank into the water. It must have gone in headfirst, for its head, sticking out just above the water, was covered with scum. Struggling to get back on dry land, it had worked itself deeper and deeper into the mud. Now it could no longer move its legs; it could only bellow in despair. A few cows stood nearby staring stupidly at the calf.

The five young people stood by for a moment staring, not knowing what to do. Their compassion, however, wasn't going to pull the calf out of the ditch. Bert, a farm boy, was the first to come up with an idea. He ran back to the gate and untied the rope that held it shut.

Then he returned to the scene of the disaster with the rope in his hand. He tied a loop in one end. This wasn't easy because the rope was bulky and stiff, but he finally succeeded.

"Now I'll put the loop around the calves neck and then we'll try to pull it out!"

"The rope is too short," objected Carl. "We can't all grab onto it."

Bert nodded. "I'll hold the rope and you put your arms around my waist. Tom will hold you; and Ina, Tom; and Miriam, Ina. Then we'll all pull at the same time."

That wasn't as easy as Bert made it sound. The calf didn't know its own best interests. When Bert threw the lasso, it jerked

its head aside so that the rope missed. The second throw missed too. Not until the third time did he succeed.

"Okay, now everybody grab hold," commanded the leader of the operation.

The others followed Bert's command. They pulled with all their might; they were so intent on what they were doing they didn't even hear the wagon with the jangling milk cans come riding up. They seemed to be getting nowhere. The calf was stuck tighter than they had thought. They didn't want to hurt the terrified animal, so they hesitated to pull too hard. They saw their hopes being frustrated.

"We'll have to pull harder," Bert concluded when they stopped for a moment. "It's for the calves own good."

Again they pulled, harder this time. The calf was being strangled by the noose around its neck; this spurred it to a sudden desperate flurry of effort, and it shot up out of the mud.

The five youngsters tumbled over backward, the rope slipping from Bert's hands. When they picked themselves up again, slightly dazed, they heard a whoop of laughter. They looked up and were staring into the face of the farmer who had chased them off his yard not half an hour ago. He wasn't alone. Two women and a man were with him to help with the milking. At the gate stood a horse and wagon loaded with pails and milk cans.

Bert and his friends were in no mood to join in the laughter when they saw their enemy. They brushed themselves off with dour looks. The farmer was still enjoying their discomfort, but at least he and his helpers were no longer laughing.

"That did look terribly funny," he said, wiping his eyes with a red handkerchief. "You children looked like a bunch of bowling pins. But anyway thanks for rescuing my calf. "

"We didn't know it was yours," Bert snapped angrily.

"No, I didn't figure you did. But if you had known, would you have left it in the ditch?"

"Of course not! That dumb animal can't help it that . . ." He stopped.

"That he has such a cantankerous owner, you mean," finished the farmer with a laugh. "Yes, my boy, I got you. But I'm not as big an ogre as you may think. You'll see."

He paused a moment and then continued, "I was wrong about you children. People who do their utmost to pull a calf out of the mud aren't vandals and destroyers. One question: did you really only arrive this past week with that dog?"

"Yes, honest! We told you that already," answered Carl, who was still offended. "You can ask my uncle."

"All right, I'll take your word for it, and I'll make it up to you. We'll go and get the dog and then I'll give you a ride back to the Wentinck farm. My helpers can handle the milking by themselves."

Suddenly the attitude of the five young vacationers changed dramatically. They were going to get back their dog! Their day had been saved.

A little later they were walking back to the farm with the big farmer. The cranky giant of a half hour ago now showed himself to be a friendly man who was very easy to talk to. When they reached the farm, Scout was immediately set free. He was wild with joy and excitement, and he danced around his companions as if he had gone berserk.

The farmer hitched a horse to a buggy and told them all to climb aboard. There was also room for Scout. Before they left, their host fetched a basket of ripe, juicy pears from the house.

"Here, this is to make up for the trouble I caused you and to give you something to do on the way. Eat them all." Then they rode off. The horse moved at a quick canter. The farmer, who was now friendliness personified, told them many particulars about the terrain they were riding through and pointed out some of the sights. Meanwhile the youngsters feasted on the delicious pears. Before they knew it, they were approaching the Wentinck farm.

Wentinck looked surprised to see his guests being brought home in a buggy. But he could tell by their happy faces that nothing serious was amiss.

"Hello there, Koppens! Did you start a taxi service?" he asked grinning, as he held out his hand to the giant.

"Only for special occasions and for very high class guests," answered their driver.

Carl told his uncle what had happened, and Wentinck confirmed that the children's story about their arrival four days ago was true. Not that Koppens needed the confirmation: he had come to know and trust the group of youngsters already. After chatting a few moments, he bade them a hearty goodbye.

Over supper the children excitedly rehashed their adventure. Everything had turned out well, but for a while they had been very worried. Wentinck, who knew Mr. Koppens quite well, had already heard the story of the slain sheep. He sympathized with the farmer's reaction, for the man had suffered a sizeable financial loss and had been sure that he had finally nabbed the culprit. Koppens was a fine fellow, but he had a short fuse.

Scout, the innocent cause of the drama, was given extra attention because of the ordeal he had undergone. Each of the five children slipped him a little tidbit from the table, and the dog took full advantage of their sympathy. So the day had a happy ending for him after all.

CHAPTER VIII

The Break-in

The next morning the weather was cool and cloudy. A couple of heavy rain showers had fallen during the night and the trees around the farm were still dripping. The children bewailed the change in weather, but Wentinck said the crops needed the moisture badly. He comforted them by saying that the sky would probably clear soon and that perhaps the sun would come out about noon.

Jake had to go into town with the wagon. "Are you boys coming?" he asked. "Then we'll stop at Barlinkhofs. If he's home, we can tell him about the note you found two days ago."

The five youngsters all shouted their eagerness to ride along and Scout joined in, barking to show his approval. Soon they were leaving in the wagon, the horse setting a comfortable pace.

It was dry out and the cloud cover was starting to break. The sun would soon be out. The air was wonderfully refreshing, and the children were glad to be out.

Barlinkhof's house was on the outskirts of the village. Jake reined in the horse and handed the reins to Bert while he jumped down to ring the doorbell. A girl answered the door.

"Is your father home?" asked Jake.

"No," said the girl. "My father is at the scene of a break-in."

"Break-in?" Jake asked in surprise.

"Yes, haven't you heard? Last night someone broke into the Rykenhoek mansion. The family went on vacation somewhere along the coast, and that was when the thieves struck. Father just left to have a look. The police are already there looking for clues."

Jake ran back to the wagon, leaped onto the seat, and urged the horse into a run. The others had heard everything. They were bursting with curiosity about this new happening.

Jake told them that Mr. Rykenhoek was a big industrialist who lived in a beautiful mansion in the village. "I saw him only last week," he said. "They must have gone on vacation only a couple of days ago. The burglar must have known when they were leaving." They were travelling at a fast clip, so they quickly reached the scene of the break-in. The Rykenhoek home was a large white mansion surrounded by a beautiful garden. At the fence that separated the garden from the street a group of villagers had gathered, who were eyeing the house with curiosity and concern. All the villagers had already heard about the break-in, and they were shocked, because nothing like this had happened in the area for a long time.

Jake jumped down from the wagon and walked toward the gate, followed by the other young people and Scout. As he started through the gate, he was stopped by a policeman guarding the house. "No one is allowed in," he said, "except those involved in the investigation."

"But I've got to speak to Mr. Barlinkhof, and he's in the house," Jake argued.

The man shook his head. "Nothing doing," he said. "I'd call him for you, but I have to stay here at the gate, or else these people will push their way into the grounds. He'll probably be out soon and then you can speak to him."

Jake was disappointed, and so were the others. They had very much wanted to find out more about the break-in. They tried to sound out the guard, but he would tell them nothing.

Suddenly Jake had an idea. He put on a mysterious air and said, "It really is very urgent that we see your commanding officer right away, because we found something two days ago that may have a lot to do with this break-in."

"Two days ago?" the policeman asked suspiciously. "But the break-in occurred only last night."

"I know," said Jake, "but there's a lot more to this than meets the eye. I can't tell you everything, but there's a lot at stake here. I will only talk to your chief," he said, trying to look important.

Tom and the others looked at each other nonplussed. Jake sounded pretty sure of himself, but what did they really know about the break-in? The guard was still only half convinced, but he didn't dare to withhold valuable information from his chief. After hesitating for a moment, he said, "Okay, I'll let you go up to the house by yourselves. But I warn you, the captain can be very ugly if you try to feed him a line."

"Don't worry," Jake said confidently, as he stepped through the gate followed by the others.

When they were far enough away from the policeman, Tom whispered, "Aren't you afraid you're going to get into trouble? After all, we don't know anything about this burglary."

"Well, I guess I did bluff him a little," admitted Jake. "But I wouldn't be at all surprised if all the mysterious events of the last few days have some connection with this burglary. So it's important that we tell our story to the chief. Besides, we have Scout with us, the best tracking dog in the country. Maybe we can be of some help."

The children had to agree with Jake on the last point. Scout's presence made them feel a little better, for they had great misgivings about their interview with the police chief. They walked along the mansion and rang at the side door. A tall sergeant answered the door, "Good morning, Sergeant Jansen," said Jake, who knew the man very well. "We'd like to speak to the chief. We have some information that may be important in connection with the break-in."

"He's on the telephone right now," said the policeman. "Come on in. I'll take you to him when he's finished."

"How did they break in here anyway?" asked Jake.

Jansen shrugged his shoulders. "We don't know much yet. The Rykenhoeks went on vacation two days ago. The housekeeper, who used to be a maid here before she got married, had agreed to come in every day to look after the plants and flowers. So she had a key. When she came here early this morning, she noticed a hole in one of the windows. And when she came in, she soon saw what had happened. The safe had been broken into and so had one of the cabinets containing the family silver. The wine cellar was also raided. They probably didn't get very much money, though, because Mr. Rykenhoek always brings everything to the bank whenever he goes away with his family. He has been notified and will probably be here in an hour or so."

The young people listened closely. Tom and Ina thought of the break-in that had happened at their house before the war and how Scout had helped capture the burglars then.

Jansen walked to the door. "I think the chief is probably off the phone by now," he said. "Wait a minute. I'll go and see."

He disappeared into the hall, and the children heard him knocking on a door. He returned a few moments later. "The chief will see you, but he doesn't have much time. So be as brief and to the point as possible." In a whisper, he added to Jake, "He's in a bad mood, so be careful."

The others overheard the whispered warning, so their hearts were thumping as they entered the large room where the chief was working.

There were four people in the room: an older woman who looked like she had been crying and who was fumbling nervously with a handkerchief; a large man in civilian clothing, whom the children recognized to be Barlinkhof; a young officer who was busy writing something in his notebook; and a quite short, broad-shouldered policeman with a ruddy face and piercing eyes. This had to be the chief. The young people stood still, a little flustered now. Only Scout appeared completely at ease.

The chief had apparently just finished questioning the housekeeper one more time. He was irritated because he seemed to be getting nowhere in his investigation and didn't have a single clue. Now he turned to the newcomers and in a stern tone he demanded, "So! And what can you youngsters tell me about this?"

Jake acted as their spokesman. "We recently found out that a strange man has been holing up in the ruins of Falconhorst castle," he said.

The chief was now paying close attention. This could indeed have a bearing on the burglary.

"How do you know?" he asked in a friendlier voice.

Jake briefly told him what they had seen after their visit to the castle. The policeman's face once more grew dark. "Adolescent fancies!" he growled. "Did you by any chance tell these children the story of Black Bertram?"

Jake coloured. "Yes, Sir, I did," he said. "But we really did see the face of a man with wild, black hair."

"Of course," mocked the chief. "Are you sure he wasn't carrying his head under his arm and didn't come right through the wall? Is that all you have to tell me?"

He was obviously in an exceptionally bad temper. But they had come this far, so they might as well tell everything. "These children also found a strange note hidden between the roots of a big oak tree in the woods," said Jake. "Tell him about it, Carl."

Stammering a little, because the piercing eyes of the Police chief made him nervous, Carl related what had happened in the woods. This story, too, seemed to make little or no impression on the policeman.

"Hmm, a note with strange letters. Probably children communicating in code," he muttered. "Anything else?"

The youngsters were afraid to say any more. They shook their heads.

Curtly, the chief said, "Thanks for the information, but I'm afraid it won't be much help." Then he turned his back to them. Disappointed, the group moved toward the door.

But Barlinkhof spoke up, "Say, these children have a topnotch tracking dog with them. He might be useful."

The policeman shook his head. "Not this time, I'm afraid. The burglar left nothing from which the dog can get his scent. Besides, it rained early this morning — probably after the break-in — so in all likelihood his trail has been washed away. This case is not going to be an easy one to crack."

Completely discouraged, Jake and his companions left the room. They felt a little foolish that they had read so much significance into their discoveries of the past two days. The tall officer led them out. He could tell by their faces that their interview had not gone very well, and he suspected that the chief had been quite hard on the youngsters.

"Don't let him bother you," he told Jake quietly. "The chief is a good man, but he has an impatient manner. He'd like to solve this case in a hurry because other strange things have been happening around here, like smuggling and such. He's burned because the burglar's tracks have been washed away."

The young people could sympathize with him. They weren't really disgusted with the police chief but with themselves. Jake was especially embarrassed. He had acted so sure of himself to the guard a little while ago. But it had been mostly bluff. It was his fault that they were now slinking away with red faces.

Reluctantly they walked through the front yard toward the gate, where the guard saw them coming back, looking obviously dejected. He laughed, and called teasingly, "I suppose the chief has deputized you children to go and arrest the burglar!"

But Jake was determined not to show his chagrin. "No, we decided to leave something for you to do," he replied. "We don't want to spoil your chances for promotion."

Tom looked back at the mansion one more time. On the wide, grandiose front door an elegant nameplate had been affixed. To the left of it, on the doorpost, painted in bold black letters was the house number: B22.

Tom started. B22? That was . . .! "Carl, Bert, girls!" he cried. "Look!" He pointed to the house number. "Look at the address: it's B22! Those were the numbers on that mysterious note. Remember? That was the only thing we could read."

The others stopped too.

"That can't be a coincidence!" exclaimed Jake. "We have to go back and tell them. This should convince the chief the note is connected with the break-in."

They hurried back and rang the doorbell once more.

"Sergeant Jansen," Jake said to the tall policeman who came to the door, "we simply must see the chief one more time. We just discovered something very important."

The man looked at them in surprise. Hesitantly he said, "Well, if you really think it's important . . . Tell you what: I'll let one of you in to see him for a minute. The rest of you will have to wait outside."

Jake started inside. Then he changed his mind. "You go, Tom," he said. "You were the one who noticed the house number."

A little frightened, Tom stepped inside. A moment later he was again standing before the police chief.

"What now?" the man sighed.

"Sir, we just made another discovery," announced Tom. "Remember that note we told you about, the one we found under the oak tree? In it there were three letters we could make out: B-2-2. And that's the number of this house."

The chief looked up in surprise. "Are you sure?" he asked.

"Yes, Sir!" said Tom, nodding emphatically. "We all studied the note. The letters B22 were very plain."

The chief whistled softly between his teeth. His bad mood seemed to have vanished. "Then that find of yours may be more important than I thought," he conceded. "We'll look into it immediately." He picked up the phone and dialled headquarters.

Now that the chief was finally convinced of the importance of their find, Tom felt quite the hero. He heard the policeman give orders to send a man and a car out to the Rykenhoek mansion right away. "Meanwhile, why don't you go outside and wait with your friends," suggested the chief in a much friendlier tone of voice. "When my man comes, I'd like a couple of you to go with us into the woods to see if the letter is still there. The car should be here shortly. I'll tell Jansen what's going on."

Outside, Tom's companions were waiting in suspense. Before Tom even said anything, they could tell from his pleased expression that this second interview had gone much better.

"The chief believes us now," he told them. "He sent for a car, and a couple of us will have to go along to point the way to the letter."

They had waited but a short while when, honking loudly to clear away the people blocking the front gate, a car came driving up to the house. At the same time Sergeant Jansen came out of the side door. "I can take three of you along," he said.

The young people looked at one another. Jake again took charge. "I have some errands to do in town. The girls can come with me; then there's just enough room in the car for the boys."

They did as Jake said, although the girls looked somewhat disappointed. The car carrying the two policemen and the three boys speeded away. The boys sat on the edge of the seat in excitement. Finally the mystery was going to be solved.

In a little while they reached the woods. They drove a little farther down a wide forest trail, but after a while the officer at the wheel said, "We'll have to go the rest of the way on foot; I can't go any farther." Fortunately the boys had been careful to imprint the location of the tall tree on their minds. The policemen moreover, also had a pretty good idea where the tree was to be found. They saw that it had rained hard in the woods, too, during the past night. The ground was still very wet.

After a quarter of an hour they were nearing the oak tree. The last few hundred metres they proceeded very cautiously, in case someone was at the tree right now. They saw no one, however. Going to the tree, Carl carefully put his hand in the space between the roots. He was taking a long time, and the disappointment grew on his face. "It's not here anymore," he said. He came up empty-handed.

Tom dropped to his knees and also searched the hollow space. Bert and the two policemen did the same. Everyone wanted to assure himself that it was so. None of them found anything. The hiding place between the roots was empty.

"I was afraid of it," muttered Jansen. "According to the chief, there was supposed to be a note hidden here that might have said something about the burglary. It only makes sense that the note was picked up before the burglary was committed."

Carefully they scanned the ground for footprints or other signs, but if there had been any, they had been washed away by the rain. The search yielded nothing unusual.

"Now let's go to the Falconhorst ruins," said Jansen. "Let' s hope we have more success there."

The boys were rather discouraged. They would have liked to show the note to the police chief to prove they hadn't just been telling stories. Jansen seemed to believe them, but they weren't sure the chief would, if they returned with empty hands. And yet they were more convinced than ever that the metal box had some connection with the break-in.

Soon they were at the edge of the forest. The old ruins rose above the heath as sombre and dark as before. The policemen seemed to know the path to the castle quite well. They reached the ancient castle gate without any incidents. The stone falcon above the gate eyed them even more mockingly than the first time.

They went straight to the room in the tower. It was empty. They also climbed the stone stairway to the second story, but that too proved fruitless. They searched the entire ruins without coming up with a sign that anyone had been there. At first the boys were quite awed by the castle ruins. The eerie face they had seen in the window for that split second was still very fresh in their minds. They half expected Black Bertram, or whoever it was, to leap out from some dark corner at any time. But when they again found nothing, their faces grew longer and longer.

“Nothing!” Bert said softly to his two friends. “I’m sure the police chief will think we made it all up.”

Jansen, who had made one last turn around the ruins, was coming back. “We may as well leave,” he said. “I don’t know whether there was some weirdo around here the other day or not. Maybe you fellows were seeing things. In any case, there’s no one around here now.”

Thoroughly demoralized, the boys followed the two policemen. When they reached the woods again, they looked back once more, in the secret hope that the strange face would again appear in the window. But there was nothing to be seen.

"I think you fellows may as well go home now," said Jansen, who could see that the boys felt like crawling under a rock. "We'll report to the chief. If he wants to talk to you again, he'll let you know."

Slightly humiliated because they were being dismissed, but also relieved because they wouldn't have to face the chief again, they said goodbye to the two officers.

Choosing the shortest route through the woods, the boys were soon back at the farm. Jake and the two girls were home too. So the three boys were immediately quizzed about the results of their investigation.

"It was a complete fizzle," Tom said disconsolately. He briefly told them what had happened.

Jake shrugged. "No doubt the police chief no longer believes a word of our story," he said. "But he's wrong. Especially because the box with the note is gone, I'm more convinced than ever that it had some connection with the break-in. And about that face we saw in the window: ghosts don't exist and we all saw exactly the same thing. I wouldn't be at all surprised if some drifter was hiding there during the thunderstorm and then broke into the Rykenhoek house the following night. And of course the man wouldn't sit around and wait until the police came to pick him up!"

Jake's words and the confident tone in which he spoke to them cheered the youngsters a little. So they hadn't been as silly and inept as they had begun to believe.

They spent the rest of the day on the farm. That afternoon they played hide-and-seek around the yard. They ran Scout through his large fund of tricks and had great fun. The break-in was almost forgotten.

But after supper, while the young people were still up, Mr. Barlinkhof came striding onto the yard. The youngsters looked a little startled to see him. Had he come with a message from the chief? They had no desire for another meeting with the stern policeman.

Barlinkhof, however, immediately made it clear that he wasn't on duty. He had only come to chat awhile with Mr. and Mrs. Wentinck, but the children were welcome to join them because he had no secrets to tell. The whole company sat down in the grass under a huge red birch, and Mrs. Wentinck poured coffee from a large metal server with a small spout near the bottom.

"What did the chief say when his men came back without the note and without having found a trace of the burglar?" asked Jake.

Barlinkhof grinned. "He grumbled a little, of course. But, on the other hand, no one really expected to find anything. I wouldn't be at all surprised if the same gang that is making a fool of customs is also responsible for the break-in. If so, we're dealing with a slick bunch."

"Is Mr. Rykenhoek back yet?" asked Mr. Wentinck.

"Yes, he drove back this afternoon. It seems that the thieves got almost no money, because it had all been brought to the bank. But they did carry off a large amount of silverware — knives, forks, spoons — all stamped with the Rykenhoek family coat-of-arms. If it turns up anywhere, it will be instantly recognized. But those thieves will probably melt it down, or bring it to a pawnshop in Germany."

"Do you have any suspects?"

"Not yet. There are a couple of suspicious characters living in this area, but we have nothing that points to them."

"Could Wasil, the gypsy, have done it?" It was Tom who asked the question.

Barlinkhof looked at him in surprise. "So you children already met him, did you? He's an unusual character all right. The police have never been able to catch him on anything, but the chief immediately inquired where he had been last night. He hadn't slept in his trailer. We found out he spent the night sleeping in some farmer's barn several hours from here. The farmer was positive that Wasil had been there all night. So he can't have done it."

Mrs. Wentinck nodded. "Wasil was here playing his violin only two days ago," she said. "And then he said he was going to make a tour of the whole area." When Barlinkhof left, it was quite late. The young guests were sent straight to bed, and the Wentincks, too, retired soon after.

CHAPTER IX

Shots in the Night

The next day was Sunday. It was much too far to walk to church and there weren't enough bikes to go around, so Wentinck hitched up the old buggy. Although he hardly used it at all anymore, he kept it in good shape. Jake had looked it over and cleaned it Saturday, so now it was ready to go.

The five young guests were, of course, delighted to be going for a ride in an old fashioned buggy. They got an early start. The weather was exceptionally beautiful. Jake was at the reins, and the children took turns sitting beside him, each taking the reins for awhile. They travelled at a calm pace. Now and then, when they were going downhill, Jake gave the spirited horse his head for awhile.

Church was held in a schoolroom filled with rows of chairs. At first the children thought it a bit strange. On the walls hung brightly coloured pictures. One of them showed a missionary chopping down a "sacred" oak tree while the pagan tribesmen looked on in fear to see whether Wodan would punish the gospel preacher. Another one showed a hall full of pompous-looking gentlemen. That was the Synod of Dort. Then there was a picture of a sea battle. You could see the Dutch admiral Maarten Harpertszoon Tromp giving orders.

Tom stared at the pictures, letting his imagination go. He imagined he was the missionary. The huge ax flashed in his hands and with a loud crack the tree came crashing down. Now those pagan tribesmen would see that their gods were nothing and that the Lord Jesus was King of the universe! The picture of the Synod of Dort wasn't as dramatic. Tom had learned about it in school, and at home his father had told him even more. The Calvinists had been forced to hold their worship services in barns and homes and had been labelled schismatics by the Arminians. But the Synod of

Dort had condemned the doctrine of the Arminians and upheld the Reformed faith, his father had said. Tom was daydreaming. Those must have been wonderful times long ago. Then you could stand up and be counted for the Lord Jesus. To be a missionary like that . . .! He would like to be a preacher, but nowadays such unusual things no longer happened. Or were the things happening now really the same as long ago . . .?

Bert elbowed him in the ribs. "What are you dreaming about? You haven't taken your eyes off those pictures since we came in. Here's the minister already,"

Tom started. The room was almost filled now. Several consistory members filed in and sat down in the front along the side wall. Behind them came the preacher, a young man, who used the teacher's lectern for a pulpit.

Tom found it much easier to listen in such a small room. The preacher seemed to be talking to him personally. He was talking about the apostle Paul, when he had been preaching to a group of women in the open air along a river. One of the women, Lydia, believed and was baptized by Paul. A little later Paul had been thrown in jail and persecution had broken out all over. And yet, said the preacher, this first open-air sermon was the beginning of the triumphant spread of the gospel which cannot be stopped. Satan tries again and again, and then sometimes persecution results so that the church is forced to meet in the open air or in barns or school rooms. But the Lord Jesus upholds His church and helps His people as long as they trust in Him.

After the church service, they rode back home in the buggy, but this time Jake took a different route. Again the scenery was magnificent. Not far from home they passed an old house-trailer standing beside the road. A man sat in the doorway smoking a curved pipe. It was Wasil. He grinned when he saw Jake and the young people.

Jake reined in the horse. "How is it going, Wasil?" he called.

"Great," said the gypsy. "The sun is shining; that's the most important thing to me." He approached the buggy and slapped the horse's flank.

Tom, who was sitting beside Jake on the driver's seat, asked him, "Did you hear anything about the break-in? Have they arrested anybody yet?"

The gypsy looked up at him for an instant. Was there a glint of suspicion in his dark eyes? Tom wasn't sure. It had been there but for a second. Then a smile spread over Wasil's face.

"What I know?" he said innocently. "I'll be just an ignorant old gypsy. But that chief — he be like a bloodhound after bear. He will get his man. Well, I go back to my spot in the sunshine." He put up his hand in greeting and then turned back to his trailer.

Jake tapped the horse with the reins and the buggy went on its way again. Tom was thinking about the strange gleam he had seen in Wasil's eyes. "I don't completely trust that gypsy," he said to Jake.

The latter shrugged. "You're probably wrong," he argued. "Wasil has been living here for years and has never done anything illegal as far as anybody knows. He makes a living with his violin."

There was little Tom could say against that. Nevertheless, a vague feeling of suspicion stayed with him.

It was a peaceful Sunday. That afternoon they again went to church in the buggy. After supper Wentinck told stories about events that had happened in this area long ago, and the group sat around listening with their ears wide open.

Monday, too, went by uneventfully. The young people went out into the fields with Jake and helped with the harvest. By nightfall they were very tired and went to bed early.

In the middle of the night Tom suddenly woke from a deep sleep. He had heard something but didn't know what. He would probably have drifted back to sleep if he hadn't noticed that Scout, too, had jumped up and was growling softly. Then suddenly BANG . . . a shot rang out in the stillness of the night, immediately followed by another.

That was it! Now Tom was sure it had also been a shot that had awakened him the first time. It sounded like it wasn't very far off.

He jumped up and shook his two friends. "Bert, Carl, wake up! I hear shots!"

Groggy with sleep, the boys sat up. Tom, who was wide awake, ran to the door in the back wall. He pulled back the latch and pushed it open.

Outside it was completely dark. The cool night air seeped into the room. The boys listened intently. The shooting had stopped, but now they clearly heard the sound of an engine. It sounded like a car was coming down the road.

"I don't think it's very close," said Carl. "The only reason we can hear it so well is that the wind is blowing toward us. It sounds like a big truck. But I don't hear any shots. You must have been hearing things."

"Listen," said Bert. "I hear another sound. There must be two trucks. Or maybe a truck and a motorcycle."

The others also listened closely. Bert was right. Now there were two engines roaring through the night.

Suddenly shots rang out again. Three, four, in quick succession. They heard the engines for a few more moments and then everything was quiet. They stood at the door listening for another five minutes or so. Scout stood beside them, his ears pricked forward, but there was nothing more to be heard.

Finally, Tom said, "Let's go back to bed, boys. Something must have happened out there. We'll get up early tomorrow morning and see what we can find out."

The next morning the boys were up early. They couldn't wait to find out what that mysterious shooting during the night had been about. But no one else on the farm had heard it. When Tom told the story to the girls, however, they were immediately ready to go out and investigate. Jake and his father were too busy to go along. The young people rushed through breakfast to be on their way as quickly as possible. As they were getting up from the table after giving thanks, a shadow passed by one of the windows. It was someone on a bicycle, but they hadn't been able to see who.

"Anybody home?" someone shouted at the door.

They all went to the door to see who it was. It was Barlinkhof. He looked jovial and excited, as he stepped into the house without waiting for an invitation.

"Is that smart tracking dog still here?" he asked. "We can sure use him."

Tom's eyes lit up, and Scout, who was standing behind the group of young people, seemed to know they were talking about him, for he uttered a happy, eager bark.

"Ah, I hear the answer already," said the customs officer, laughing. "Scout is volunteering for duty."

Then he turned to Tom. "Would you come along to handle the dog?"

"Of course!"cried Tom.

The others immediately chimed in, "Can we come too?"

Barlinkhof hesitated. So many sightseers at an official investigation might be frowned upon.

Looking at him beseechingly, Tom pleaded, "Scout really belongs to all of us, you know."

Laughing, the officer gave in. "All right," he said. "But remember: no noise and obey all orders promptly. And, of course, if we find anything you're to keep it under your hats. This is an important case."

"What happened anyway?" asked Wentinck.

"We had a good catch last night and with Scout's help we hope to make it even better," Barlinkhof said mysteriously. He paused a moment as they all waited in suspense. Then he gave them a short account of what had happened.

Because there had been so much smuggling in this area over the last few months, the police and the customs officials had begun stopping all vehicles that passed through this area, even when they didn't enter the forbidden border zone. Last night Barlinkhof and one of his fellow officers had been stationed at a crossroads some distance from town and a few kilometres from the border.

A truck had come along, and when the officers signalled for it to stop, it had barrelled down on them with its engine roaring, almost running them down.

Taking out their pistols, they had opened fire on the fleeing truck, to no effect. They had come to the checkpoint on motorcycle. Jumping onto the seat, they went after the truck.

The chase reached breakneck speeds. The truck driver must have known the roads very well, for he took even the most dangerous corners at amazing speeds. He had finally skidded into a narrow country road. But the two men on the motorcycle knew the roads well too, and soon they were catching up to the truck.

They tried to pull alongside it but couldn't, because every time they tried, the truck tried to force them off the road.

Taking out his pistol, Barlinkhof had then opened up at the truck's tires, shooting over the shoulder of his companion, who was driving the motorcycle.

Barlinkhof's audience was hanging on his every word. When he paused, they stared at him, waiting for him to finish.

"And then?" Jake asked impatiently.

Barlinkhof laughed somewhat painfully. "Then my buddy and I almost paid dearly for our efforts. They shot back at us from the truck. But they missed. Then all of a sudden something was tossed from the back of the truck.

"My partner hit the brakes, but it was too late. We went flying head over heels with the motorcycle. Did we ever take a nasty

spill! My partner was even unconscious for a while, and I sprained my left wrist." He pulled up his sleeve, displaying the bandage.

"And did the truck get away?" Tom asked, disappointed.

"No, it didn't. One of my last shots had hit one of the tires. When I scrambled up after my painful tumble, I saw the truck skid sideways all of a sudden and then plunge into the ditch. The truck lights went out and the cab door slammed. I figured the men inside must have taken off on foot, but I couldn't see a thing in the dark. And I had to check on my partner first. He had an awful gash in his head and was unconscious, but he soon came to. When he saw that the truck had come to a stop, he wanted to go right over to it, but he could hardly walk. I helped him to the side of the road and set him down against a tree. The motorcycle still worked."

"What had you run into?" asked Ina.

"You wouldn't guess in ten times," said Barlinkhof, "so I'd better tell you. It was a huge sack of coffee beans. Apparently the smugglers tossed if off the back of the truck to stop us. It didn't do them much good, however. The sack had burst and there were coffee beans all over the place. When I saw what it was, I immediately knew we were on the right track.

"I climbed back on the motorcycle and drove up to the truck. I was a bit leery about doing it, because if those men were still around, I was a sitting duck. But nothing happened. The truck was deserted. It was loaded with bales of coffee. Then I drove to a nearby house to find a telephone. My partner was picked up and brought to the hospital. He's doing pretty good. And the truck was, of course, impounded. But the smugglers escaped, and now we need Scout's help to track them down. Come, it's high time we were going. I'll tell you more later. Now our time is precious."

Meanwhile, Tom had fastened a leash to Scout's collar. The group of young people followed the officer, brimming with expectation. They struck out along a narrow path that skirted the woods and farmlands; it was the most direct way to the spot where the truck had left the road.

Although he had been up all night and had taken a nasty fall, Barlinkhof was bright and alert. Finally he was on the trail of the smugglers. Now headquarters could no longer accuse them of lying down on the job or of being in cahoots with the smugglers.

"Do you have something Scout can get their scent from?" inquired Tom.

"Yes, I have," said the officer. From his pocket he pulled something that had been carefully wrapped in wax paper. "This is a cap that belongs to one of the men in the truck. In their hurry to get away they left it lying on the seat."

After a half hour's march, they came to their destination. The place where the truck had skidded into the ditch was still clearly visible, but the truck had, of course, been hauled away.

"Look," said Barlinkhof, pointing. "You can still make out their tracks here because they cut across this plowed field. But farther on the ground is harder and you can't see their footprints anymore. Now let's see if that dog of yours can do better than we can."

At just that moment a car came speeding up the road and stopped parallel to the group. The door opened and out stepped the chief, followed by Sergeant Jansen. The third man, sitting behind the wheel, was the local constable who had been with them when they had searched the castle. The chief gave them a friendly greeting, but asked Barlinkhof, "You think it's a good idea to have all those children trailing along? They'll just be a nuisance, and if we catch up to those hoods, they'll really be a bother."

"I figured they'd be of some help," replied Barlinkhof. "The dog will probably perform better among friends than strangers. And these boys have shown that they can handle themselves all right in a pinch."

The children blushed at this bit of praise and were very pleased to hear the customs officer taking their part. He now took out the cap, an old, frayed thing, and held it under Scout's nose. As soon as the dog had smelled it, he leaped over the ditch and took off across the plowed field, following the footprints. Tom held the leash and the others followed him.

It was an exciting journey. The trail led across the fields in a huge arc. Now and then in marshy ground they found more footprints. Scout never hesitated for a moment, sometimes he pulled so hard on his leash, Tom could hardly hold him. Slowly they were coming closer to the large forest along the border zone. The fugitives had apparently made a wide detour to avoid any houses and to cut down their chances of running into police or custom officers.

Now the men and young people were fighting their way through a field overgrown with thick brush. They had been going for over an hour, slogging over rough terrain and jumping across drainage ditches. Miriam and Ina especially were very tired, but they didn't dare complain, because they were afraid they would be sent back.

A path became visible in the underbrush, and Scout followed it. He hurried forward and a few minutes later they were in the woods. On they went between the trees. They were all very curious where they would end up, and the children in particular actually expected a couple of men to pop up in front of them at any moment. Again the trail turned in another direction. Scout headed straight toward a dense mass of bushes growing under the trees. The branches snagged their clothes and scratched their hands and faces. Suddenly Scout lunged forward and Tom lost his grip on the leash. The dog shot ahead.

Tom didn't dare call Scout, because he was afraid the smugglers might be somewhere nearby. Barlinkhof, who was fighting his way through the tangled growth alongside Tom, said half aloud, "We're running into a dead end here. The river should be straight ahead of us."

A little later they heard Scout barking. They hurried forward and in a few moments they reached the place where the dog was standing. Underneath the overhanging trees and the bushes flowed a wide, murmuring stream. It was the small river that the children had already come to know, but here it was considerably wider. Barlinkhof and Tom were the first to reach the German shepherd. The rest of the group, however, wasn't far behind.

Scout stood on the riverbank. The footprints of the fugitives were very clear in the soft ground. But this was all there was to be seen.

"They must have waded the river here," said Tom. "I'm pretty sure their trail comes out on the other side."

The chief meanwhile was walking along the riverbank searching for clues. He pointed to a piece of rope tied to a small tree. "I think there was a rowboat or canoe tied up here," he said. "You can see the indentations it made in the mud. The smugglers must have cut the rope in their hurry to get away. Just take a look."

It was easy to see that the rope had been cut with a knife, and in the wet ground along the bank the marks where the boat had been pulled up on land were plain to see. The young people looked at one another in disappointment. The fugitives, it seemed, were going to get away after all.

With a great effort, they followed the river for a ways — first upstream and then in the other direction — in the hope that Scout would pick up the scent elsewhere. Some distance upstream, where the river was shallow, they waded across and continued their search on the other side. But they found no further trace of the fleeing smugglers. Looking very glum, the chief had to admit that the criminals had gotten away.

The children, of course, were sorry Scout hadn't been able to catch the smugglers. But this time the chief remained friendly.

"Your dog did a good job," he said, scratching Scout's head. "If they hadn't had a boat stashed here, we would've caught them for sure."

Barlinkhof was deep in thought. "I don't understand it," he said, shaking his head. "Where can they have gone? That boat wasn't tied here by accident. They seemed to know where they were headed. They must have a hideout somewhere around here, I should think. But I know this area like the back of my hand . . . Well, at least we've got a truckload of coffee. Did you find out who the truck belongs to?"

"The license plates are phony. We did find out that much. And as you know we didn't find any papers. Still, I'm sure we'll eventually find out where it came from. At least we have some clues now. The truck is parked in that unused fire department garage on the edge of the woods."

"Is that safe?" Barlinkhof asked worriedly.

The chief shrugged. "What could go wrong? I don't have room for a truck like that at the police station. The place is well padlocked and hardly anyone knows that the truck is parked there. Besides, it's only for twenty-four hours."

The two policemen and Barlinkhof, all a little downcast, headed back toward the village. The young people headed in the opposite direction, through the woods toward the Wentinck farm. It was a long walk, and they were very tired when they finally arrived. Mr. Wentinck and Jake weren't home, but Hanna and her mother immediately asked them whether Scout had found the smugglers. The children told them what had happened, pointing out that Scout had done his work well in spite of the fact that it had come to nothing.

Mrs. Wentinck shook her head. "They must be a clever bunch," she said. "And this area has always been so peaceful: nothing ever used to happen here!"

The young vacationers spent the rest of the day around the house. They secretly hoped that Barlinkhof or one of the policemen would suddenly show up to tell them that they had picked up the trail again and that they once more needed the services of Scout. But the day went by without any further incidents.

CHAPTER X

Fire!

The boys slept very soundly that night. The next morning the sun had been up for a long time and still the room in the loft was silent. Only Scout was awake, but he lay with his head on his forepaws blinking sleepily.

Tom was dreaming. He was driving the motorcycle, with Barlinkhof on the back. He was holding onto the handlebars for dear life as they sped after the smuggler's truck at speeds up to 100 kilometres per hour. The trees went whizzing by on either side and Tom took the corners at perilous speeds. They were drawing closer and closer to the fleeing truck. The smugglers seemed to be very frightened, for they kept honking the horn. But Tom wasn't going to be scared off. He accelerated even more. Barlinkhof, however, wanted him to slow down and he kept shaking Tom's shoulder. But Tom only bent lower over the handlebars. He would show those smugglers! Now Barlinkhof was tugging at his arm and shouting his name. What did the man want, anyway?

Reluctantly Tom opened his eyes, blinking in the morning light. He saw Jake bending over him. "Wake up, Tom! There's a fire in town!" he said.

There was the sound of the horn that Tom had heard in his dream. He almost lapsed back into it. But no, now he was wide awake: it was the wailing of a fire siren!

He was out of bed in a single bound. Carl and Bert were also just awake and were busy dressing.

"If you boys hurry, I'll give you a ride into town on the wagon," said Jake. "I'd like to see where the fire is myself."

They were ready in an instant. When they came outside, Ina and Miriam were already standing there laughing at them because they had slept so late. "We almost left without you," teased Miriam. "What a bunch of sleepy heads." The boys grinned sheepishly. The girls had been a step ahead of them this morning.

Jake fetched the horse from the barn and quickly hitched it to the wagon. Just as they were about to ride off, Mrs. Wentinck came running out with a bagful of sandwiches and a pear for each of them. "Something to eat on the way," she said. "I don't want you going into town on an empty stomach."

Then the horse set off at a fast trot while the young people dug into the bag of sandwiches and fruit. The wail of the fire engine had stopped. No doubt the firemen were already busy fighting the fire. Before they were even out of the woods they could see the red glow between the trees.

"It must be close to the edge of the woods," Jake said thoughtfully. "Maybe it's Geertsema's farm or Banning's house. Although it looks like it's even closer."

The road turned and soon they could clearly see the scene of the fire.

"Well, I'll be . . .!" exclaimed Jake. "It's the fire department garage! I wonder how that caught fire. I thought it wasn't being used anymore."

"The fire department garage?" asked Tom. "The chief said something about it yesterday. What was it?"

"That's where they parked the truck loaded with coffee — the smugglers' truck!" cried Carl.

They had now reached the edge of the forest. Jake reined in the horse and tied it to a tree. Everyone jumped down from the wagon including Scout, who seemed as excited as the others. They trotted toward the burning building.

Quite a few spectators had already gathered and were being kept at a safe distance by two policemen. The large garage was a mass of flames, which was little affected by the streams of water aimed at it from the fire truck. Jake made conversation with some people who had arrived on the scene earlier.

"That garage has had it," observed an old farmer. "Good thing the sparks are being blown away from the woods. If it was blowing the other way, we would probably have a forest fire on our hands."

"How did it happen?" asked Jake.

The farmer shrugged. "It must have started about half an hour ago," he said. "Suddenly flames were shooting up through the roof. But don't ask me how it started."

In the meantime, Tom had spotted Jansen, who had been with them yesterday when they were tracking the smugglers. He was assigned to keep the people back, but he had little to do because the people hung back on their own. When Tom and Scout approached him, he gave them a friendly nod.

"Is the smugglers' truck caught in the fire, too?" Tom asked softly.

Jansen looked startled. "How did you . . ." he began. Then he laughed. "Oh, that's right, you were with us yesterday when the chief mentioned it. Yes, the truck is still inside. But the funny thing is, it's empty."

"Empty?" Tom echoed, finding it hard to believe. "What about all those sacks of coffee?"

The policeman pulled up his shoulders and spread his hands, palms up. "I guess I can tell you, since you're involved in the case already. Maybe we'll need that dog of yours again. But, remember, don't blab it about!"

Tom nodded, indicating that he would keep it to himself, and Sergeant Jansen told his story: "As you know no one was guarding the garage, because the chief didn't think there was any danger. But early this morning, Geertsema, the farmer who lives yonder, suddenly heard a loud bang, like an explosion. It came from this direction, and when he looked this way, smoke was already beginning to curl from the roof of the garage. He ran over here with his hired hand, but by the time they got here, the place was already in flames. The main doors were unlocked. When the men opened them, they found the truck — empty. The explosion seemed to have happened in the truck, for it was in the heart of the fire and the fire had spread from it to the building. A man coming by on his bike called the fire department and the police, while Geertsema and his man tried to put out the fire, but it had already spread too far."

"But who do you think started it, and who could have taken the coffee?" asked Tom, still finding it hard to understand.

The sergeant bent over him, whispering confidentially, "That gang of smugglers must have gotten wind of the fact that their load was stashed here. So during the night they hauled it away.

Then they placed an explosive with a slow fuse in the truck. When the truck exploded, the whole garage caught fire."

"But why did they do that? For revenge?" Jansen shook his head. "That may have played some role," he said. "But I suspect they did it primarily to destroy the evidence. The chief planned to trace the truck to its owner, remember. But now the evidence is gone."

Now Tom understood. He thought of what Mrs. Wentinck had said yesterday: "They must be a clever bunch." This showed how right she was.

The fire was beginning to slack off a little now because it was running out of fuel. The garage was burned almost to the ground and the metal skeleton of the burned truck was clearly visible inside. The crowd was starting to break up, as the firemen were just mopping up now.

Tom found his companions again, and they were just about to turn back to the wagon when someone called them. They looked around, and close to the smoking remains of the fire, they saw the chief talking to someone. He motioned to Tom.

Tom and Scout walked toward him, while the others stayed behind and waited.

Apparently the chief's self-confidence had received a painful blow by this morning's events. This time he wasn't at all overbearing, but acted friendly, almost conspiratorially. "Those hoods have outwitted us again," he said. "But we're not about to give up. And I need you and Scout to help collar these characters. Can I count on you?"

"Of course!" said Tom.

The chief signalled to Jansen and another policeman and told them to send the remaining spectators home. Most of them had left already anyway. Then he turned back to Tom. "The smugglers emptied the truck during the night and then set it on fire. A bold stroke! And they must have had quite a few men, because they didn't load the coffee onto another truck, but apparently carried it away on their shoulders. You can see their trail through the pasture over there. Then it turns left to the woods. I ordered my men to keep the spectators out of that area so they wouldn't erase the tracks. But I'm sure we won't be able to see their tracks once we get into the woods: that's where Scout comes in."

Tom nodded. He was beginning to like the chief. "Can my friends come too?" he asked.

For a moment the policeman hesitated. Then he said, "I'd like to say yes, because you and your dog have helped us a lot. But this time I would rather not take your friends along. That gang doesn't have such a large head start on us, and if we catch up to them, we might be in for a nasty fight. I can't expose a group of children to such danger. With you I'll make an exception, because you're the dog's master."

Tom felt sorry for the others, but he had to admit that the chief was right. He walked back to the wagon and told his friends what was up. They were very disappointed, but all they could do was get on the wagon and go back with Jake.

Tom took a piece of twine from the wagon and fastened it to Scout's collar. As the others rode off, he reported back to the chief, who had three men with him. They cut diagonally across the pasture, following the trail, which was quite plain here. Soon, however, they were on the edge of the woods. The gang had used a small trail that wound through the trees and bushes deeper into the woods. So at first it wasn't hard to follow the men's tracks. But after a while the ground became harder so that they could no longer see footprints.

Now they came to a place in the trail where it branched off in three directions. For a moment they stopped, not sure which one to follow. But Scout seemed to have picked up the smugglers' scent, for without hesitating he turned up the path farthest to the right. The others followed.

A moment later the dog stopped and sniffed at something lying on the path. When Tom bent down he saw several coffee beans in the grass. He pointed them out to the chief, who was delighted.

"One of the sacks must have a hole in it," he said. "Now we know for sure we're on the right trail. Let's hurry."

Because they were looking for them, now they kept finding coffee beans on the trail. The chief laughed humourlessly. "Those men aren't as smart as I thought they were," he remarked. "They've left a clear trail behind them. This time we could follow them even without a tracking dog."

They followed numerous trails, both narrow and wide, through the woods for about half an hour. The smugglers must have known the woods very well in order to find their way in the dark. Scout never hesitated for a moment, and here and there a few coffee beans showed that the German shepherd was still on the right track.

Tom was in a cheerful mood. The chief's remark that they could have done without Scout this time had grated on him, but at least now they had a good chance of catching the criminals. As they turned down another path, Tom was surprised to see the chief's face suddenly clouding over. A few minutes farther down the trail, Sergeant Jansen muttered half aloud, "Oh-oh, this doesn't look good. We're heading straight for the river again."

"Quiet!" snapped the chief. "Those men might be nearby."

But his expression and the tone of his voice showed that he had already come to the same conclusion. They continued a little farther and then they reached a small clearing between the trees. In front of them was the small river.

In the soft bank they could still see the place where the thieves had dropped their heavy sacks. The grass had been trampled and the marks of a boat that had been tied here were also plain to see. But the boat, the thieves and the sacks of coffee beans had vanished. The river streamed by murmuring quietly as if it knew the secret but was unwilling to tell.

"You'd almost say it was magic," said Jansen. "Those smugglers come and then disappear, and we can' t seem to put our hands on them."

The chief paced back and forth angrily in the small clearing. He turned red and pale by turns, and sometimes he seemed about to jump into the water.

"Those slippery packrats!" he suddenly exploded. "They've outsmarted us again. The coffee is gone, the truck burned, and the whole gang has disappeared without a trace. The story will be in tonight's papers and the whole country will be laughing at me. Those skunks! But I'll get them." He shook his fist and kicked the grass.

“Should we follow the river a ways and see if we can pick up a trail elsewhere?” asked one of the men.

“What?” grunted the chief irritably as he stood racking his brains. “No, that won’t do any good. We did that yesterday without any results. There’s only one thing we can do. I’ll ask for help at the district office and then we’ll get a large squad of police and customs officers to scour the woods and both banks of the river. We’ll turn up something eventually.”

“Can Scout and I help too?” Tom asked somewhat timorously.

But the chief was in a bad mood again. “No,” he said. “I don’t need children underfoot. And I don’t need that dog of yours either. If only they’ll give me enough men, I’ll break this case wide open.” He turned to his men and said, “Come on, let’s get back to town.”

The policemen began to retrace their steps. Tom was left behind with Scout. Tears of anger and disappointment burned in his eyes, he was so wounded by the chief’s snappy answer. Scout seemed to sense his master’ s grief. He pushed his head against Tom’s hand and gave him a loyal and sympathetic look.

“It’s not fair!” Tom said in a low voice. “We did our best and now the chief acts as if it’s our fault that those hoods got away. Just wait, I’ll . . . I’ll . . .” But what could he do? After he had thought awhile, he began to calm down. First he had better cut through the woods and get back to the farm. But he couldn’t get the idea out of his mind to get the jump on the police chief and track down the smugglers by himself — today.

He had no idea how to go about it. All kinds of fantastic plans flitted through his mind. Until a suddenly plan popped into his mind that did seem practical.

His face brightened, and as they neared the farm, he stroked Scout’s head and whispered, “We’ll solve it together — you and I. I have a great idea.”

The dog, seeing his master in a good mood again, happily barked his agreement.

CHAPTER XI

The Black Pool

After lunch, the day became very hot. The young people were sapped by the heat and stretched out on the grass in front of the farmhouse in the shadow of the sprawling birch.

Tom, however, was not with them. He was rummaging about in the barn loft where he and his two friends slept every night. He dug several things out of his suitcase and put them into his pockets. As he was closing the lid, his eye fell on a flashlight. He hesitated a moment and then he grabbed it too and put it in his pocket. It might come in handy if he was late in returning.

He climbed downstairs and whistled for Scout. Together they stalked across the backyard of the farm, past the beehives and through the small vegetable garden. At the rear of the garden began a small path that led through the bushes to a creek about twenty metres beyond. Some distance from here, the creek emptied into the river that flowed through the woods.

In the water lay a small boat, a kind of canoe. It belonged to Jake. Tom, who had some experience canoeing, had taken it out for awhile several days ago. The canoe was tied up and the paddle — one with a blade on both ends — lay in the bottom. Carefully Tom stepped inside. Steadying the boat along the bank, he coaxed Scout into the back. Then he untied the rope, and the slender craft slid forward over the swift water.

Tom felt a little guilty as he paddled away. He hadn't asked Jake if he could use the canoe nor had he told anyone of his plan. After the disappointments and unsuccessful ventures of the past two days and the harsh words of the police chief, he had struck upon a plan that he wanted to try out all by himself. He didn't want anyone else to know. If it, too, failed, at least he wouldn't be embarrassed. Nevertheless, he wasn't entirely easy with his decision. Inwardly he knew what he was doing wasn't really right. But he drove the thought from his mind and dug in with the paddle so that

the canoe went shooting ahead over the surface of the water like a racing shell.

Scout sat motionless in the back. He seemed to sense that any unexpected movement on his part would make the boat capsize.

After about ten minutes or so the creek slowly widened and then spilled out into the river. Tom let the canoe drift with the swift current. If he had figured right, in about fifteen minutes he should be reaching the place where the smugglers had loaded the coffee on a boat to vanish without a trace.

His plan was simply to follow the same course on the river that the crooks must have followed. If he kept his eyes peeled, studying both banks, perhaps he would see something that would put him back on the track.

For now, there was nothing to be seen, but Tom was enjoying his expedition tremendously. He felt as if he were floating through an enchanted forest. The tall trees met high above the water to form a long green archway. The sun shone between the leaves and cast dancing spots of yellow light on the water. The current was swift enough that, even when he didn't paddle, Tom made good time.

He kept looking left and right, listening to every sound. Occasionally a fish jumped near the boat. Birds flitted from branch to branch, and twice he saw squirrels peering curiously from behind a tree.

Soon he was passing the spot where the two smugglers who had fled from the truck had launched their boat. And about one hundred metres farther downstream he came to the spot where the coffee sacks had been loaded. Now Tom was more watchful than ever. He felt like a genuine scout. He would uncover the smugglers' trail before the police and customs officers went to work.

The boat floated on. Tom was again using the paddle to go a little faster. Both banks were now lined with dense, thorny bushes. Tom grinned to himself. The chief would not have an easy time of it tomorrow if he wanted to search this terrain.

Suddenly the river took a sharp turn. Skilfully Tom maneuvered the boat around the bend. He was now coming to an area of the forest where he had never been before. When he was through the turn he saw that a few hundred metres ahead the river widened into a small lake.

Now Tom remembered what Jake had told them about the Black Pool, a mysterious pond through which the river flowed. The water of the Black Pool was supposed to be very cold. Jake had gone swimming there once, but hadn't liked it. The water was sulphurous and felt oily. There were also stories that the Black

Pool contained dangerous whirlpools that could pull down even excellent swimmers. Jake hadn't seen any, but his father had forbidden him to swim there ever again.

So this pond just ahead had to be the Black Pool. As the canoe headed toward it, Tom felt a strange tightness in his chest that he couldn't explain. For the first time he regretted not having told someone of his plan. For a moment he thought of going back. But immediately he shook off the thought and, thrusting hard, he paddled the boat onto the dark water of the small lake. He was struck by the strange atmosphere of the place. A leaden stillness hung over the Black Pool, and the water looked dark and threatening. Tom felt uneasy. He paddled faster to reach the other end of the lake, where the river narrowed again. The current was swifter than he had expected here. The canoe skimmed forward over the black surface.

In the middle of the pond there seemed to be a small island. The island itself wasn't really visible because it was surrounded by a deep border of reeds, but out of the tall reeds rose a couple of trees and a few bushes. So there had to be land.

Tom steered the boat close to the reeds, but saw nothing unusual. Suddenly the canoe was rocking wildly, as Scout sprang to his feet. He was holding his nose to the air, growling angrily. The sudden motion scared Tom, for it had tilted the slender craft dangerously. He was just about to order the dog to settle down, when Scout suddenly coiled himself and leaped toward the island, landing in the water. Tom hadn't expected the sudden lunge, and suddenly he, too, found himself in the water. The canoe had capsized.

First he thrashed about in panic with his arms and legs. Surfacing, he gasped for air. Then he got a grip on himself. Brr! The water was icy. He had swallowed a little of it and tasted the peculiar sulphurous tang.

Tom was a good swimmer, but the thought of the whirlpools Jake had mentioned made him uneasy. He looked around. The canoe had already been swept some distance away by the strong current going through the lake. Should he swim after it? But then he might be caught in a whirlpool. He decided to swim to the nearby island first. After that he would see. When he turned on his other side, he saw Scout emerging from the reeds. The German shepherd had swum to the island, but seeing what had happened to his master, he came swimming back to help.

"Go back, Scout!" cried Tom, happy to see his loyal companion. "I can make it by myself." With a few hard strokes he reached the dog, and together they set course for the reeds.

Soon Tom felt ground underfoot. With difficulty he fought his way through the reeds. One glance was enough to show him there was nothing unusual on the island. Most of it was covered with tall grass and in the middle stood a few trees and bushes.

"First I'd better take off my wet clothes and dry them," he told himself. "When I swim to shore I'll tie them in a bundle and hold them over my head. My expedition is over anyway. I hope the canoe isn't lost."

Quickly he undressed and spread his clothes to dry in the bright sun. Meanwhile, Scout kept jumping excitedly around his master as if trying to get Tom to chase him.

"Wait a minute, you clown," said Tom. "This is no time to play. I'm surprised at you — jumping out of the canoe that way. I thought you knew better!"

Scout seemed to hear the note of reproach in his master's voice, but he didn't seem to pay much attention. He was a bundle of excitement, and after a while it became clear to Tom that the dog had discovered something. He followed Scout across the island and saw him disappear into the reeds.

"What do you think?" grumbled Tom. "That I'm going to start tramping around in those reeds without any clothes on?"

Hesitantly he took a couple of steps between the tall stalks. Then he discovered the reason for Scout's excitement.

Through the reeds ran a narrow channel which was not visible until he was on top of it. And in the channel a boat was anchored.

Tom flushed with surprise. Immediately the smugglers came to mind. Could this be the boat they had used? He went to the craft. It was empty and was tied to a small stump. Alertly Tom studied the area. In the boat lay four oars and a long pole.

"Strange," mumbled Tom. "Where could those men be? There's no one on this island. I guess I'd better take another look around."

Suddenly he saw something that gave him a scare. In the bottom of the boat lay several coffee beans. Now there was no doubt about it: the boat had definitely been used by the smugglers. But where could they have disappeared to? Had they perhaps hidden this boat in the reeds and then taken a rowboat to shore? In any case, he resolved to give the island and the reeds one more close search before he left. Maybe he would find more clues.

After taking another look around the boat, he waded back through the reeds to the island. First he would put his clothes back on — at least if they were dry. Fortunately the sun had done its work. The clothes were almost completely dry and Tom quickly began dressing.

Meanwhile, Scout was sniffing around on the island. Twice he came back to Tom and tried to get him to follow, but Tom warded him off, laughing. "Wait a minute, Scout," he said. "Let me finish. You must have caught the scent of the smugglers, but those men are long gone by now. It won't do us any good."

The dog remained anxious, however, and when Tom was dressed, Scout ran ahead of him to the middle of the island, to a dense clump of prickly bushes. Apprehension began to grow in Tom. Was someone hiding there?

Cautiously he circled the bushes, peering through the leaves. There seemed to be an open space inside which was surrounded by the dense growth. Ah, here was a narrow path leading inside. Scout shot ahead of him. Tom followed very cautiously.

As he had thought, in the middle of the bushes was a small clearing. It was covered with grass, and although the grass was trampled, that was all he saw. Nevertheless, Tom felt very jittery. A strange excitement made his heart beat faster. He felt as if he were on the verge of discovering a dark secret.

Again he looked around. No, there was nothing to be seen. But what was Scout doing?

The German shepherd had gone to the middle of the clearing and clamped his teeth on a big clump of grass.

Tom looked at him in surprise. He had never seen Scout act so strange. Tugging hard, the dog pulled the grass right out of the ground. It came up in a neatly cut, square sod, which had apparently been lying there loose.

When Tom stepped forward and looked into the hollow underneath, to his surprise he saw a heavy, rusty iron ring. He stooped and, taking hold of it, tried to pull up on it. But the ring was stuck.

Strange! As he pulled again, he heard a peculiar grinding noise. The next moment the ground under his feet was sinking away.

CHAPTER XII

The Secret Passage

At first Tom hardly realized what was happening, but this lasted only for a few seconds. Then he saw. The entire centre of the clearing was sinking, and Tom and Scout were sinking with it. They descended about three metres and then stopped. They were standing at the bottom of a wide shaft like a huge well. The walls were made of massive stones cemented together, but in the bottom of the wall was a large opening about half the height of the wall. Inside the opening Tom could see the beginning of a stone stairway leading downward.

Hesitantly he peered into the darkness. His heart was racing wildly. He knew that he had made a tremendous discovery, which would undoubtedly solve the mystery of the smugglers' sudden appearances and disappearances.

What should he do? Explore a little farther with Scout? That might be dangerous. Perhaps it would be better to turn back and get help from the police. But when he looked up, he realized that he had no choice. The sides of the well went straight up without any footholds. He couldn't climb out. He was trapped!

Fear rose in his throat. But when he looked up at the blue sky, he felt himself growing calmer. God was watching him, and He would be watching him even when he went down into the tunnel. For a moment Tom folded his hands and closed his eyes.

Then with new resolve he turned around and started down the stone stairway, followed by Scout. The stairway was steep and the stairs narrow. At first Tom descended very carefully, but when all went well and he heard nothing from below, he speeded up. That was a mistake. When he had almost reached the bottom of the stairway, his foot slipped and he lost his balance. Frantically he clawed the air trying to catch himself. His right hand fastened on an iron bar protruding from the wall. His feet left the stairs and for a moment the bar was bearing his full weight. It moved a little, but then held firm.

He found his footing again and was about to descend the last few steps, when he suddenly noticed that it was becoming darker on the stairs. He looked up, and what he saw frightened him horribly.

The large stone platform covered with sod was slowly rising. The entrance was closing behind him.

In panic he began to scramble back up the stairs, but he was too late. Diving for the iron bar, he furiously tugged at it. But it wouldn't budge and the opening remained dark. Sobbing, Tom stood surrounded by an inky darkness.

As he stood there, frightened and despairing, he felt Scout pushing his head into his hand. The dog had apparently noticed that Tom was troubled and was trying to comfort his master. He licked Tom's hand, and jumped up on his hind legs to show his sympathy. It did, indeed, help his master. Tom was ashamed of his tears and overcame his panic.

Only a few minutes ago he had been confident of God's care, and now, at the first setback, he was already giving way to despair. But this total darkness was terrifying. Suddenly he thought of the flashlight he had dropped into his pocket at the last minute. He hoped it hadn't been ruined by the water! It was supposed to be waterproof and he had recently put in new batteries.

Nervously he reached into his pocket, took out the flashlight and flicked the switch. A bright beam of light flooded the tunnel. Immediately Tom regained his courage. His situation didn't seem nearly as desperate now. Playing the light about him, he sat down on the bottom stair to think.

What should he do next? It must be possible to make that stone platform descend again from this side. But how? And what good would it do him? He couldn't climb out of it anyway. There was only one thing to do: see where this underground passage took him.

At the foot of the stairs began a long tunnel in which he could just walk upright. The floor was quite smooth and also seemed fairly level. Tom aimed his light beam down the passage, lighting up the rough, gray walls. They seemed to make a sharp turn where the light petered out.

Heaving a deep breath, he stood up. His enthusiasm for his scouting expedition had worn thin, but he couldn't stay here. From his pocket he took a piece of rope which he tied to Scout's collar. He wanted to keep the dog close beside him. Then together they advanced down the dark passage. Scout was very calm and seemed not to be bothered at all by his grim surroundings.

Once he had started out, Tom felt his resolve returning. Every nerve in his body was taut, for at any moment he might run into the gang of smugglers, who were obviously making use of this hidden passage. At the same time, he was counting on Scout to give him plenty of warning if danger were approaching.

The walk down the passage posed no problems. When Tom neared the sharp turn, he switched off his flashlight so the glow of the light would not give him away. The utter blackness, however, again filled him with fear. He literally couldn't see his hand in front of his face.

Groping along the wall with one hand, he shuffled forward step by step. To Scout the darkness seemed to be no problem at all, and Tom was glad he had him on a leash. It seemed ages to him before he rounded the corner. Finally he felt the corner under his hand.

He stood very still and listened very closely. The tunnel seemed to go on, and Tom could hear nothing. Finally he dared to turn his flashlight back on. In the glow of the light he saw a new section of the tunnel stretching out ahead of him, empty and endless.

He had decided to see it out to the end, so he hurried on. He had to be careful, however, because the floor was very rough in places. Suddenly he tripped and the flashlight flew out of his hand. The darkness closed in on him. Panic rose high in his throat as he groped about on the rough stone floor. Had it broken? Where was it? He crawled ahead and his fingers closed on the familiar shape of the flashlight. Tom was almost afraid to try it. His fingers touched the glass. It wasn't broken! Fearfully, he pushed the switch. The light blazed on, dazzling him.

Shakily he scrambled back to his feet. Now he proceeded more carefully. Sometimes the ceiling of the tunnel was so low, he had to stoop to go on. Twice he came to other tunnels that branched off to the side. But when he shone his light down them, he saw that they ran dead after a short distance.

Again the main passage turned and then went on. The air was damp and musty: it smelled like wet dirt. Slowly Tom was beginning to feel as if he were being smothered. Actually he was buried alive down here. He couldn't go back. And the tunnel seemed to be endless, and who knew what was waiting for him around the next bend? Perhaps death!

Suddenly he felt incredibly tired and sank down on the floor to rest. If only he hadn't been so foolish as to go off all by himself! If he didn't return, no one would have the slightest idea where he was. He felt tears welling up in his eyes, but he resisted them and stood up again. What he had done was not only foolish but also wrong. Only the Lord could help him now.

Once again he rounded a bend in the tunnel. Then to his relief he noticed that the passage was beginning to climb. He took it to mean that he was nearing the end. The suspense was building up in him. Again he switched off the flashlight and stood perfectly still. At first he could see nothing, but when his eyes became used to the darkness, about fifty metres down the tunnel he saw a weak glow, as if a light were shining through a small crack somewhere.

Tom's heart raced wildly. Quietly he stalked toward the light. When he was about ten metres away, Scout uttered a low, threatening growl.

"Hush, Scout!" whispered Tom, almost inaudibly. He stroked the dog's head and felt the fur on his neck bristling. That was a sure sign that his four-footed companion sensed danger ahead.

Tom moved on, step by step. Now he thought he could hear a muffled babble of voices. He had finally reached the end of the tunnel. It was blocked by a heavy door. The door stood slightly ajar. Through the small crack filtered the light from the brightly lit room beyond.

A cry of surprise almost escaped Tom when he peeked in and saw part of the room. He recognized it! It was a round room with stone walls, along which stood a stone bench — the tower room in Falconhorst castle where they had taken shelter from the thunderstorm!

When he looked closer, however, he saw that he was wrong. As far as he could see, this room had no windows at all, and although it was midday, the only light in the room came from the lamp.

His attention was now captured by the sound of the voices he had heard earlier. At a large round table, which Tom could see only

partly, sat several men. From his angle Tom could see three of them, but from the sound of the voices he could tell that one or two more men were sitting on the other side of the table.

They seemed to be quarrelling about something. Tom heard a big, blond fellow, whom he could see very clearly, arguing loudly, "Sure, we're doing all right now. But sooner or later someone's going to catch on."

Tom was startled to hear that the man was speaking German. At the same time, however, he realized that the man wasn't himself German, for he was speaking with a Dutch accent.

From the other side of the table a voice with a ring of authority spoke in clipped tones, "Remember, Hendriks, there is no room for cowards in our organization. An S.S. man does not despair or give up! Remember that!"

"Yes, Herr Oberst," answered the blond man meekly.

Tom's earlier surprise gave way to even greater amazement. The man who had spoken with such authority was obviously German, and the whole group were S.S. — ex-soldiers. Oberst meant commander. So they were lead by an ex-Nazi officer! Tom seemed suddenly to have been transported back into the wartime and the occupation. But that was impossible. The war had been over for a whole year!

The German who had been addressed as Herr Oberst spoke again, but this time less harshly. "We must keep this operation going until next year," he said. "If we can expand our smuggling operation over the coming fall and winter, and if we can do a few other jobs on the side, by next summer we should have enough money for all of us to emigrate to South America and start new lives. I know where we can get excellent forged papers."

One of the other men spoke up. "It's a good plan," he said, "and of course I'm all in favour of keeping it up. But our chances of getting caught are increasing. A few days ago those cops on the motorcycle almost nabbed us. If I hadn't tossed that sack of coffee off the back, my comrade and I might not be here now."

"Well, you know your orders," replied the leader. "We try to avoid bloodshed if at all possible. But to avoid capture shoot to kill if you have to. Anyone who gets caught and spills our secret is a dead man." The man's voice again had that hard, steely ring. Tom shuddered to hear it.

At that moment the hooting of an owl sounded from somewhere above the room where the men were sitting. It was repeated three times. Then followed a deep hush, which was again broken by three hoots.

"That's Wasil," said the leader. "Better open up."

Tom started in surprise at the name of the gypsy. So he belonged to the gang after all! His surprise became even greater when he saw what happened. One of the men stood up and walked to a stone stairway, which Tom could just see from where he was. The man did something that Tom couldn't follow, and suddenly in the apparently solid ceiling of the room a trapdoor appeared.

Someone lowered himself through the hole and descended the stairs. Sure enough! It was Wasil. The trap door closed above him in the same mysterious manner.

In the few seconds that it was open, however, Tom had made another astonishing discovery. The trapdoor opened into the tower room of Falconhorst castle. The room in which the smugglers were hiding was the underground counterpart of the other.

The leader of the gang, who was still outside Tom's field of vision, addressed the gypsy angrily. "What's the idea of coming here in broad daylight?" he demanded.

Wasil grinned. "But my noble Sir, it is for you I do this," he said servilely, but without sounding very impressed by the commander's sharp words. "I have for you important news."

"Couldn't you have put a note under the big oak?" asked the leader. He sounded less angry now.

Wasil shook his head. "I was being afraid you would not get it timely," he said. "I take very, very great care when I come here. Nobody see me come to the castle."

The commander was silent for a moment. He seemed to be satisfied with Wasil's answers. "Well, what's the important news?" he finally asked.

"Tomorrow many police and border men come to look in the forest," Wasil told them. "Mr. police chief ask for many more men from the city, and they will, as you say it, comb the forest."

The leader uttered a mocking laugh. "Let them come!" he jeered. "That strutting little chief is too dumb to be any danger to us."

The old gypsy grimaced. "I think maybe you are right," he said. "But I say to myself, 'Wasil, better you tell the captain. You never know what happen.' And there is one thing more. On a farm close to here some children are staying, and they have with them a fine tracker dog. The farmer tell me many stories about him. This dog and his boy — maybe they are more dangerous than all those many policemen."

"Then we must get rid of the dog," the leader said in a hard voice. "You can see to that, can't you?"

Wasil shook his head. "I do not kill," he said. "And such a fine dog — it would not be right. But I know how to make dog come. We take him. We train him. For a dog like that we have many uses, yes? I will try. But I have one more news. I have another job for you."

"That's good news," the leader grunted eagerly. "Tell me about it."

"It is the big white house I tell you about before," said Wasil. "An old woman live there with her son and a maid lady. A man works there also. But he goes home after every day. Tomorrow night the son goes to a wedding party in another place. He will come back not until the next day. The maid lady sleeps upstairs, and the old woman doesn't hear too good or walk too good. So tomorrow is a good night to make the job. Right?"

The leader thought a moment. "Are you sure that hired man won't stay overnight to keep an eye on the two women?" he asked. "And are you sure the old woman keeps lots of money around?"

The gypsy grinned. "I am a good spy," he said. "I learn much. The son — he don't like me. One time he chase me with pitchfork from the yard. He will pay for it, to treat this old gypsy like that! But I talk to his working man out in the garden. He is not too fast in the head, you know, and he tell me everything. Look, I draw a map of the house. I even know where you must find the money."

As he spoke, Wasil pulled a large sheet of paper from his inside pocket and spread it on the table.

Tom, still standing at the door had heard everything. The entire setup was now clear to him. He was trembling with suspense and outrage, but his curiosity was stronger than his fear. As Wasil was flattening the floor plan on the table, Tom very carefully opened the door just a little farther in order to see better.

The men around the table had stood up to look at the drawing. The leader, too, bent forward over the table so that his face suddenly came into Tom's view. Tom started in shock. It was a pale face with a mass of black hair — "Black Bertram," he mumbled.

Tom was so startled, the hand on which he had been leaning slipped and he fell forward against the door, which hurled open. The members of the smuggling ring jumped in fright as Tom tumbled into the room. But even before he could scramble to his feet, two men were already on him, shouting and cursing.

CHAPTER XIII

In the Dungeon

Tom tried to fend off his attackers, but be didn't have a chance against the two strong men. Suddenly, however a dark blur shot over him. It was Scout: seeing Tom threatened, he launched himself at the two hoodlums. He clamped his sharp teeth into the forearm of one of the men, who uttered a howl of pain and let Tom go. At the same time Tom landed a punch in the middle of the other man's face so that he staggered back momentarily. Tom turned and ran for the door. But before he could reach it, the other members of the gang were on him.

The next moment a flailing tangle of bodies was rolling about on the floor, almost burying Tom and Scout completely at times. The two brave companions gave a good account of themselves. Especially Scout showed himself to be a dangerous opponent. But they were vastly outnumbered and outweighed. In a few moments the boy and the dog had been overpowered and trussed up with ropes so they could hardly move.

The only one who hadn't participated in the fight was the old gypsy. He had retreated to the other side of the room where he had looked on impassively. The leader with the dark, wild features was again sitting at the table. Two other men were binding up wounds made by Scout's sharp teeth. Another man brought Tom to the table holding a pistol in his neck to prevent any escape attempt.

Tom, however, hadn't the faintest notion of trying to escape. With his hands tied, he had no chance anyway. He was bruised and sore from the fight and felt utterly exhausted. His knees were shaking and he had to fight to keep from bursting into tears. If only he hadn't been so foolish as to go off by himself! He knew what was in store for him. "Anyone who gives us away is a dead man," the leader had said. And if that applied to members of the gang, it certainly applied to someone who was spying on them.

The German commander was speaking. "Take that chair," he told Tom in a rather friendly tone of voice. Tom was surprised but tried not to show it and quickly sat down on the chair offered him. Exhausted as he was, he was glad to be sitting.

"You're a brave fellow, and I respect you for it," the man said. "But you have heard and seen far too much, so we shall have to kill you. First, however, I'd like some information from you. What's your name?" Tom pressed his lips together and said nothing.

An ugly expression came to the commander's face. For a moment he looked as if he were about to jump up and attack Tom. But he restrained himself. "We have ways to pry loose your tongue, sonny boy," he hissed at Tom. "But right now I have other things on my mind. We'll put you away somewhere safe for the time being and I'll deal with you later. But you can be sure you're not getting out of here alive."

Turning to Wasil, he asked, "Is this the boy and the dog you were talking about?"

The old gypsy had been staring fixedly at the boy all the while. Was there a hint of sympathy in his eyes? Now he looked at the commander and answered, "Yes, but I must ask you, don't kill the boy. You keep him locked up for a little time. Later we see what we do. We must keep his dog, yes, but . . ."

"Shut up, Gypsy!" snapped the leader. "I give the orders here, not you. Your fear of bloodshed might cost you yet!"

Wasil retreated into the shadows, but his dark eyes flashed back and forth between Tom and the ex-S.S. officer. He did not look very pleased with the turn of events.

The commander barked an order to two of his men. One of them seized Tom by the collar, and the other grabbed the rope with which Scout had been tied and dragged the dog away after him. The two prisoners were taken to a door which looked just like the door Tom had fallen through, but it was a different one. Behind it was another long passage.

Tom, who had not yet given up the idea of escaping, observed carefully where they were going. Side by side on the left of the passage were several heavy iron doors. The first of these was opened with a large key, and Tom and Scout were shoved into the dank, dark space behind. The cell door clanged shut, the key grated in the lock, and the footsteps of the two men retreated back down the tunnel.

Tom had been shoved so hard, he had fallen, and for several minutes he lay on the ground half dazed. He felt hopelessly abandoned. Tears oozed between his closed eyelids. All was lost and he was going to end his days miserably in this dark dungeon. The chill of the damp stone floor seeped through his clothes, and he shook with sobs. After awhile, however, he calmed down. His hands, first clenched in desperation, now opened and folded together. In his dark, underground cell Tom prayed for deliverance. How long he lay this way, Tom had no idea, but finally he was completely at peace. His body still ached all over, but he was no longer sobbing. Scout lay near him. The dog was still trussed up, but he seemed not to have been seriously hurt in the struggle.

Suddenly Tom heard footsteps. It sounded like several men trudging past his cell. They didn't come from the underground tower room, but from the other direction, so the passage must have another exit. Tom heard the door to the underground chamber open and the men go inside. Apparently they left the door ajar, for he could hear the voices of the gang members quite clearly. They seemed to arguing about something. Tom tried hard to hear what they were saying.

Once he thought he heard Wasil's voice; immediately thereafter the S.S. officer shouted, "Don't you contradict my plans, you gypsy beggar!" A little later the voices became quiet. But the knowledge that the gypsy disagreed with the commander gave Tom a little hope. He squirmed over to the wall and sat up with his back against it.

Again footsteps sounded in the passage. A key grated in the lock and the door opened. As a light was shone on his face, Tom tried to see who was behind the flashlight. He hoped it was Wasil, but he was disappointed. It was one of the other crooks who had come to bring him a jug of water, a piece of bread, and a gray blanket.

"Here's something to eat and a blanket to sleep under tonight," said the man. He flung the blanket in one corner of the cell on a wooden bunk, which Tom noticed now for the first time. The man didn't look evil tempered, so Tom decided to risk asking him a favour.

"I can't eat this way," he complained. "My hands are tied." He held up his hands, which were bound at the wrists.

"Hmm," grunted the man. "I guess that's hardly necessary in here; there's no way you can get out of here anyway. Okay, hold out your hands." He pulled a knife out of his pocket and cut the ropes off Tom's wrists. Tom almost asked him to cut Scout loose too, but he just caught himself. It was better if he didn't draw attention to the dog. He could untie Scout himself pretty soon. He thanked the man, who turned and left without another word, carefully locking the door behind him. As soon as he was alone again, Tom reached into his pocket. Good, the flashlight was still there. He snapped it on and went to Scout. The dog wagged his tail joyfully.

Tom had a hard time untying the ropes that held the dog. He had a jackknife in his pocket, but didn't want to cut the rope. He would need it to retie him later, so that the men wouldn't see what he had done. But at least tonight Scout needn't be bothered by the ropes. The loyal German shepherd was overjoyed when he could finally walk again. He pranced around the cell, and Tom, fearing the dog would start barking with happiness, had to admonish him very firmly.

Together they disposed of the piece of bread Tom had been given. Scout ate most of it, because Tom wasn't very hungry. After a long day filled with strong emotions, he felt drained. It was evening by now, he guessed. His eyes were heavy and his head was spinning. Stretching out on the wooden bunk, he called Scout, who snuggled down beside him. Tom pulled the blanket over both of them, and it wasn't long before he slipped into a deep sleep.

When he finally woke up again, he had the feeling that he had slept for a very long time. He was right, but he had no way of knowing whether it was night or day, for the cell remained completely dark.

Scout had crawled out from underneath the blanket. Tom heard him pacing back and forth. He switched on his flashlight and saw a new piece of bread lying beside the water jug. So someone had been in the cell as he slept. He supposed that he had slept through the morning. Perhaps it was around noon already. Scout looked hungry, but the well-trained dog had not touched the bread while his master was sleeping. This time Tom, too, was hungry. He felt much better after his long sleep. Together they devoured the bread, and Tom poured some water into a hollow in the stone floor for Scout.

Meanwhile, Tom tried to hear what was going on in the underground chamber. But all he could hear was the muffled murmur of the men's voices. Later he thought he also heard the clink of glasses and the pop of corks, and he surmised that a drinking party was in swing. The voices soon became louder. At first they sounded rather jovial, but after awhile the talk died out completely and, to his puzzlement, the underground room fell silent.

As he sat asking himself what the gang was doing, Tom suddenly heard the sound of quiet footsteps outside his cell door. The lock squeaked and the door began to turn on its hinges. In the doorway appeared the shape of a short man, carrying a flashlight. It was the old gypsy. Tom stared at him, nonplussed, wondering what was happening.

Wasil gave him a big grin. "Hurry, you come with me," he said. "This dark is no good. Us gypsies — we like the sun. I think you, too, like the sun much better than this, eh? Come, I show you the way out."

"But . . . but . . ." stammered Tom, "what about the other smugglers? If they see us . . ."

The grin on Wasil's face became wider. "They sleep like bears in winter," he said. "Come, we go now quick. The dog too. We talk more later."

Tom wasn't sure whether he was awake or dreaming, but he hurried out of the cell with Scout behind him. Wasil closed the door again.

"You wait here," he whispered to Tom. "I come back quick. I bring back the key first."

He padded down the passage and disappeared through the door leading into the underground chamber. When the door opened, Tom smelled booze and heard the snores of the sleeping men. The gypsy was back in a minute. He took back the flashlight, which he had left with Tom, and led the boy and the dog down the long passage.

By now Tom was sure this was no dream and that he was really being freed. His head was spinning and he was burning with curiosity. First he had seen Wasil as an enemy and now suddenly the gypsy was acting like a friend.

They had been walking for quite some time. This tunnel seemed to be even longer than the one Tom had come through the first time. Otherwise, it looked exactly the same. Tom, who was following Wasil very closely, could no longer restrain himself. "What happened?" he asked. "Where are we going? What time is it? Is it still daytime?"

"You have much questions," the gypsy answered teasingly. "It is a whole day since when you fall through the door. Soon darkness will come. What happen? That big shot captain — he tell me I stay here. He don't trust this gypsy no more, because I say he no kill you and he no kill the old woman in the white house. I think maybe he's going to keep me here a long time away from the sun. But to keep old gypsy a prisoner is no easy thing. I always come ready: I keep powder in my pocket. When I open the bottles for my friends, I put a little powder in the wine. They sleep many hours."

Tom listened with amazement. Wasil was a wily old fox! But many more questions leaped to his mind.

"Why were you helping Black . . . I mean . . ."

The gypsy laughed. "So you hear the story of the castle and the ghost already, eh? Yes, he look like Black Bertram, I guess. But this not be him. Why do I help him? There is much to tell.

"In the wartime many gypsies are put in concentration camp and die. They grab me one day too. The man they bring me to is this captain man of the smugglers. He find out I was born in south Russia and he begin to talk Russian with me. He was born in Russia himself. We talk about old days, and he like me, so he let me go.

"After the war is over, I see him again one day, and he asks me many questions, and I tell him much. I do not know what he is doing first, but slowly I find out. Then I know if this old gypsy say something, goodbye gypsy."

“That note in the metal box under the oak tree, the note about Mr. Rykenhoek’s house — did you put that there?” Tom asked all of a sudden.

Now it was the gypsy’s turn to look surprised. “You find that? But how you know what it say? I write in Russian!”

"I could only make out the B22,” said Tom. “That was Rykenhoek’s address.”

Wasil nodded. “Yes, I copy it from the door,” he said. “I did write it. Rykenhoek, that big, rich man — he never give me no money when I play for him. One time he sic his dog on me. So I say to myself, I hope someday someone steal all your money. Yes, I tell the captain about this rich man.”

Tom said nothing. He didn’t know what to say. What Wasil had done was wrong. To avenge himself on those who hurt him seemed second nature to the gypsy. But Tom knew it wasn’t right. Jesus had said, “Love your enemies.” Should he talk to Wasil about it? Tom didn’t really dare — not here in this underground passage.

Suddenly Wasil stopped and turned around. “We talk enough now,” he said. “We are close to the end, so no more talk. It comes out in a lonely place, but we got to be very careful.”

“Why? Are there more members of the gang around?” Tom asked in a whisper.

“No,” replied Wasil. “But this tunnel comes out in Germany. When the Germans catch us, we have much trouble.”

They walked on in silence. In a few minutes Wasil stopped again. They had apparently reached the end of the tunnel, but Tom couldn’t see any sign of an opening. The gypsy, however, knew his way around. He went to a corner of the passage, lifted a metal hook and pushed with all his might.

Suddenly a bright shaft of sunlight struck Tom’s eyes. Wasil pushed the heavy door that blocked the tunnel entrance farther open.

“Follow quick,” he said to Tom, extinguishing his flashlight.

Blinking in the bright daylight, Tom stepped outside, followed by Scout. The gypsy closed the door again. They were standing on a steep slope covered with grass. Several metres below them lay a valley where cattle were grazing. Looking behind him, Tom could see nothing of the tunnel entrance. It was covered with grass.

"How do we get down?" he asked Wasil. The hill dropped down very steeply in front of them.

"Not so hard," said the gypsy. "We have nothing to carry; we have no trouble. Smugglers have much trouble here. This be how they move things over . . . I mean, under the border to Germany. Each time they must carry it down this hill too. Most times they slide it down on ropes."

As he talked, Wasil was already starting the downward climb, putting his feet in small footholds chopped into the slope here and there. Tom followed him. Once he caught on, it went rather easy. Soon he was standing on level ground.

Scout of course couldn't climb down in the same way, so he had hung back. When he saw that his master was down, however, he also came sliding down the slope, taking the last few metres in one long jump.

"There," said Wasil. "So far so good. Now we must go away from here very quick. Here is lonely country. Only one or two farmers sometimes come here, and one of them helps the smugglers. Better he does not see us."

They cut across the valley, climbed a hill on the other side, and then found themselves in a hilly terrain covered with trees and bushes.

"Here is safer," said the gypsy. "Now you must listen to me very good. From here you must find your way by yourself. I don't go no farther."

"Why not?" asked Tom, his heart plummeting. "Aren't we going to the police?"

Wasil flashed a grin. "You go to the police. And if you listen good to what I say, you catch the smugglers. But I go far away now. They are bad men and they will kill me for what I do. I don't wish to die."

"But at least help the police catch those crooks first," pleaded Tom.

Wasil shook his head. "You forget. The policeman will put me in the jail too, because I help to smuggle. I like it better to be free. Tonight I sneak back over the border, get my horse and trailer, and I go far away. It be a big world and a gypsy is home wherever he can be free."

Tom sighed. He could see that Wasil was determined to do as he said.

"Now listen good," continued his rescuer. "See where the sun goes down? That is west. When you walk that way, you come to the border pretty soon. But watch out for the German police. Don't let them catch you. When you are on the other side, go quick to the police. Two men of the gang are going now on the way to the De Wit farm to make the break-in tonight. The rest sleep for a long time yet in the big room. But later tonight the powder will no longer be strong. The police must get them soon. You have been in the big room in the tower? Good! You take the police there."

"We hid there once during a thunderstorm," said Tom. "But how do you get into the underground room?"

"At the bottom of the stone stairs, one of the stones in the wall, has another colour. All the stones are dark gray, but this one is blue. Push it hard. It moves, oh, maybe twenty centimetres; then, poof, a trapdoor opens in the floor to the room underneath. When you know it, it is not difficult."

The gypsy repeated his instructions once more. Then he shook hands with Tom and said goodbye. Tom felt strange. Wasil was a smuggler and a thief, but he had also risked his life to save Tom's.

"Thank you, Wasil," he said, faltering a little. "May things go well with you."

The gypsy turned left and melted into the bushes. Tom and Scout purposefully set their course west. They made poor time in the hilly, bushy terrain, but at least Tom felt fairly safe. He didn't want to run into anyone, so he studied the area carefully from every hilltop to make sure the road ahead was safe. When he came to the top of one of the higher hills, about one hundred metres ahead of him he saw a paved road. On the other side of it, the terrain changed into fairly level heartland. He went on, but his discovery worried him greatly. How was he going to find cover in the open field? He would be spotted for sure!

Soon he reached the end of the wooded terrain. In front of him lay the paved road. He was about to cross it, when he heard the sound of an engine approaching. He shrank back into the bushes. A minute later a jeep drove by carrying two English soldiers and a civilian.

When he heard the jeep stopping a little farther down the road, he edged forward in order to get a better look. Now he saw that several hundred metres to the right the road was blocked by a barrier. Beside the barrier stood a small customs house. In front of it strolled two English soldiers and two other men. The Soldiers were no surprise to Tom because he knew that this part of Germany was still occupied by England.

But he couldn't possibly cross the road here and continue across the field without being seen. What should he do? Should he walk up to the soldiers and tell them everything?

But Tom was sure they wouldn't believe him right away. His story sounded too fantastic. They would probably hold him until tomorrow. By then the burglary would have been committed and the gang members would have revived. Discouraged, he sank to the ground. Had he come this far only to fail? Suddenly he felt how tired he was and how his stomach ached with hunger.

The sun was settling below the horizon and slowly twilight was creeping in. How long would it be before it was dark enough for him to go on without being seen?

He waited with Scout beside him. Hours seemed to pass before twilight began to turn into darkness.

The jeep drove by again going in the other direction. A light flicked on in the customs house. Somewhere a dog barked. Very slowly the minutes dragged on.

Finally Tom decided it was dark enough. He had grown stiff from waiting, and first he stretched his arms and legs. Now he had to be on his toes. He whispered a few words of caution to Scout, who replied with an intelligent look.

A moment later two gray shadows flitted across the road and melted into the darkness of the heath.

CHAPTER XIV

In the Minefield

At the Wentinck farm, the disappearance of Tom and Scout went unnoticed at first. Limp from the heat, the children spent the early afternoon lying in the shadow of the large birch tree in front of the house. Later Mrs. Wentinck called them in for a cold glass of buttermilk, and that was the first time they asked what had happened to Tom.

No one knew. Bert had seen him and Scout near the beehives after lunch. "I think he went out with Scout to look for those smugglers once more," he said. "He seemed to be embarrassed because Scout hadn't found anything."

When Tom still hadn't turned up at suppertime, however, everyone began to grow uneasy.

After supper the five young people began searching in the vicinity of the farm. They shouted Tom's name but got no answer. Jake was the one who discovered the canoe was missing. Now the uneasiness turned into fear.

Ina turned pale and started crying. "Maybe he drowned," she sobbed.

"Of course not," Carl consoled her. "Tom is a good swimmer and Scout is with him. He can swim even better."

Darkness was falling. Mr. Wentinck was very anxious now. He took out his bike and rode into town to tell the police about Tom's disappearance.

He returned about an hour later. "I spoke to the chief," he said, "and he told me that he would do his utmost to track Tom down. But he can't do anything tonight. Tomorrow a large squad made up of policemen from the city and customs officers will be here to help. They're going to search the woods and the whole area for signs of the smugglers, and then they hope to pick up Tom's tracks at the same time."

That night no one got very much sleep at the Wentinck place. The two girls wept, and the others, too, struggled with fear and anxiety.

The next day the police and customs men scoured the woods from one end to the other. But although they made a very painstaking search, they found nothing unusual. Toward afternoon the news came that in the village a capsized canoe had been spotted floating down the river. Someone had pulled the craft ashore. Jake was immediately driven to the location in a police car in order to identify his canoe.

Yes, it was his. There was no longer any doubt that something very serious had happened to Tom.

The Wentinck house was filled with dismay. Ina and Miriam roamed about with tear-stained faces, and the boys, too, were pale and quiet.

At suppertime Mr. Wentinck prayed fervently for Tom's safe return. They feared he was dead and Mr. Wentinck felt he had to inform Tom's parents.

Just before dark, Barlinkhof came cycling onto the yard. He had helped in the search and was in a glum mood. They still hadn't found a single clue. "We'll continue our search tomorrow," he said. "But to tell you the truth, we scarcely know where else to look. The men from the city are staying here overnight so they can start again early tomorrow morning. I'm not going to bed at all myself. Today was really my day off and tonight I'm on border patrol."

He said goodnight and left, looking sombre. He was blaming himself for having involved the boy and the dog in the case. Perhaps if he hadn't, the boy would still be alive. Now chances were those hoodlums had grabbed the boy and perhaps had already killed him.

In this gloomy state of mind he arrived home. He quickly had a bite to eat and went out again. He struck out into the woods with his partner, until they reached the eastern fringe of the woods. Here they hid themselves in a spot overlooking a large heath that stretched across the German border. Usually this area was only lightly patrolled because the customs men didn't think the smugglers would risk using such an open field. Moreover, this area had never been cleared of booby traps and land mines planted during the war, so everyone avoided it. In the last few days, however, Barlinkhof had begun to suspect that perhaps for that very reason the smugglers were running their goods through here.

The minutes dragged by. Both men spoke only occasionally and then in whispers. It was now completely dark and the moon rose in the eastern sky.

"I don't think we're going to have much success here," Barlinkhofs partner said quietly. "In half an hour or so, if the sky remains clear, the moon will be shining right down on this field. Then no smuggler will be foolish enough to venture out on the heath."

Barlinkhof said nothing. Although he knew his partner was right, he still didn't want to leave. He stared hard across the dark, deserted field. Did he see something moving on the eastern edge? He stooped down so he could look the field over from ground level with the bright night sky as background.

Yes, he saw it again: a dark figure was stealing toward them across the minefield. Or were there two figures? He wasn't sure, and he gently nudged his partner. "Look down low. Something is coming," he hissed.

The other officer stooped too. Together they watched in suspense as the two shadows slowly came closer and closer. The one looked considerably larger than the other.

Barlinkhof was feeling rather pleased with himself. They were finally about to capture two members of the smuggling ring, and maybe they would be able to solve the whole mystery. He was so eager that he jumped into action a little too soon. When the figures were about twenty metres away, he leaped forward and barked, "Halt!"

For a second one of the figures stood frozen in fright; then it whirled and fled. The other, however, calmly stayed where it was. Now the officers saw that the second figure wasn't a man, but a dog.

"Halt or I'll shoot!" Barlinkhof shouted, even louder. He seized his revolver as his partner switched on a bright flashlight.

And then in the strong beam of the flashlight Barlinkhof saw something that made his heart leap in astonishment and joy. The dog did not turn and run but came straight toward them, and that dog was . . . Scout!

Immediately Barlinkhof realized that the fleeing figure had to be Tom. And he had almost shot at the boy! "Stop, Tom! It's me, Barlinkhof!" he yelled as loud as he could. "Don't move! You're in a minefield."

The figure fleeing across the heath had already put some distance between himself and the patrol, but suddenly he stopped, hesitating.

Again Barlinkhof shouted his name. Now Tom, too, recognized the voice which Scout had immediately recognized as a friendly one. He turned around and walked back toward the two men. A moment later Tom and the two officers were face to face, while Scout circled them, wagging his tail.

Barlinkhof reached out to the boy with both hands. "Boy, am I glad to see you alive!" he said heartily. "You've had us worried sick! Where did you come from? And what are you doing walking around in a minefield in the middle of the night?"

Tom was having a hard time putting everything together. "So I'm not in Germany anymore?" he asked. First he had thought he was being stopped by German customs.

"No Sir!" said Barlinkhof, laughing. "You're back on home ground. But it isn't very safe ground around here. We're right on the outskirts of an uncleared minefield. You cut straight across it."

The moon was now well above the eastern horizon, and to give the boy a sense of where he was, Barlinkhof pointed toward the dark ruins not far away, which were now clearly visible in the bright moonlight. "See, that's Falconhorst. Now do you recognize the place?"

Bewildered, Tom stared at the black ruins. Finally he realized where he was and the danger he had been in. But he had no time to dwell on it, for suddenly all the things that still had to be done tonight rushed back into his mind. Hurriedly and confusedly he began to tell the men what had happened: his discovery of the smuggler's hideout, his capture, and his escape. As he spoke he gradually calmed down.

The two customs officers listened with growing amazement. When Tom was finished, Barlinkhof said, "If any other boy told me that story, I'd think he was making it up. It's a good thing I know you and know you aren't one to spin out fantasies."

They spent a few minutes planning what to do next. Barlinkhof took charge. "First we'll go to Falconhorst," he said, "and tie up those hoodlums before they wake up. If the sleeping potion has already worn off, we're in for trouble. But from what the gypsy said, I think we're still in time."

They quickly made their way along the edge of the woods. The moon was now shining brightly, so they had no trouble following the path. Finally they turned up the trail that led to the castle.

The ruins loomed up before them, huge and threatening. The stone falcon above the gate looked eerie in the moonlight. Cautiously they crossed the courtyard and crept through the ruined corridors and rooms of the castle until they reached the tower door.

Here they stopped for a moment, listening. Tom jumped at a sudden noise, but it turned out to be a bird that they had startled. Barlinkhof carefully opened the door into the tower chamber. Again they stopped to listen. But everything remained quiet. The other officer shone his flashlight into the room. It revealed nothing unusual: the room was empty. They breathed easier and stepped inside, playing the light along the stone benches, the stairway, and up the stairwell. Sure enough, there was the blue stone Wasil had mentioned.

Barlinkhof walked over to it and pushed against it. The stone slowly slid back, and all at once a trapdoor opened in the floor. A faint glow shone from down below. Apparently the lamp in the underground chamber was still burning. A smell of smoke and alcohol came up through the hole. They could hear the snores of the sleeping smugglers very clearly.

"Everything is all right," whispered Barlinkhof. "Our knights of the underground chamber are still sound asleep."

Quickly he lowered himself through the opening. The other two followed him, and Scout, too, jumped down without hesitating.

In the stuffy underground room, seven of the smugglers lay in a drugged sleep, some with their heads on the table and others on the floor.

"We'll have to tie them up, but where are we going to find that much rope?" said Barlinkhofs partner.

Tom had the answer. "See that cabinet in the corner?" he said, pointing. "There's a big coil of rope inside it. I know because that's where they got the rope to tie me up." He walked to the cabinet and opened the door. The coil of rope was still there.

Swiftly they went to work. While Tom cut the rope into the required lengths, Barlinkhof and his partner tied up the hoodlums one by one. Then they rolled them onto the floor and frisked them. Scout stood by, keeping a wary eye on the others, ready to attack the first man that offered resistance. But none of them woke up. A couple of them made some disconnected moves in their sleep and mumbled a few words, but Wasil's sleeping potion was so strong, they couldn't shake off their stupor.

Half an hour later the task was finished. The two officers sighed with relief. The most dangerous part of their job was behind them.

"Now we have to contact the police," said Barlinkhof. "This bunch has to be picked up, and someone has to get to the De Wit place as quickly as possible before those two hoods make their move and maybe kill those two women."

They conferred briefly. They decided that Barlinkhof, Tom, and Scout would go to town as quickly as possible to contact the police. In the meantime, the other officer would keep watch over the trussed up prisoners.

"Are you sure you'll be all right here, all by yourself?" Barlinkhof asked his partner.

The man laughed. "You better get moving," he said. "Don't worry about me. These crooks won't get loose, and if I get any unwelcome visitors, I have not only my own revolver, but these weapons as well." He pointed to the table on which lay a collection of guns and knives taken from the prisoners.

"Okay, Tom, then let's go," Barlinkhof said eagerly. "Can Scout make it through the trapdoor?"

Tom smiled. "No problem," he said. He climbed up the stairs, and at the top he stooped as if playing leapfrog. "Jump, Scout!" he said.

The clever dog caught on right away. Taking a good run he leaped up on Tom's back, and then, as Tom staggered under his weight, he launched himself up through the trapdoor opening in one swift bound. Then Tom hoisted himself up into the tower room, with Barlinkhof close behind him. After shouting one last farewell to the man remaining behind and promising to return as quickly as possible, they hurried off.

Outside, the moon was now high in the sky, so they had no trouble finding their way. When they reached the edge of the woods, Barlinkhof said to Tom, "We've got to get our hands on a bike or something, otherwise it will take us way too long to get to town and warn the police. Not far from here on the outskirts of the forest there's a little shack. An old poacher lives there all by himself. Maybe we can find a bike there."

Barlinkhof knew the area very well. Tom would have lost his way dozens of times in the dark woods, but the experienced officer never hesitated for a moment. He strode on, followed by Tom and Scout. After about ten minutes, they came to a small house. It was little more than an old shack. It was dark and quiet.

"Looks like the old poacher and his dog are out hunting," muttered Barlinkhof. "Otherwise that dog of his would have raised the roof by now."

When they checked, they found the doghouse beside the shack empty. Tom was disappointed, but Barlinkhof said calmly, "No matter. I didn't want him anyway. All I want is his bike, and that should be around here somewhere."

He stepped to the back door and tried the latch. The door wasn't locked and they could walk right in. Barlinkhof switched on his flashlight. The shack consisted of a single room. In the middle of it stood a wobbly table and one chair. In one corner stood a bed covered with dirty bedclothes. Leaning against the far wall was a new-looking bicycle.

"Good," said Barlinkhof, taking the bike and wheeling it outside.

Tom thought it somewhat brazen to walk in uninvited and borrow someone's bike. But when he expressed his feelings, the customs officer chuckled. "That old poacher has caused the law plenty of trouble," he remarked. "Now he'll make up for it by lending us his bike."

He closed the door behind him and jumped on the bike. Tom climbed on the rear carrier.

Barlinkhof pedalled hard. Fortunately the bicycle had a bright headlamp on it. They went whizzing between the trees and bushes. Several times they came very close to falling, but each time they caught themselves and kept going. Scout ran behind them.

It was not long before they arrived in town. Without letup Barlinkhof raced to the police station. Stopping, he threw the bike against the wall and sprinted inside. Sergeant Jansen was sitting at the desk, nodding sleepily. No other policemen were around.

"Hey, Jansen!" cried Barlinkhof. "Look who I found: the boy we've been looking for all day, Tom Sanders."

All at once Jansen was wide awake. "Where on earth did you come from?" he asked in surprise.

Tom was about to answer, but Barlinkhof interrupted him, "He can tell you all about it later. To make it short, Tom and his dog have found the smugglers' hideout. What we need right now is a good number of policemen to round up the whole gang. But there's no time to waste. What's the chiefs number?"

The astonished sergeant gave him the phone number. Barlinkhof went straight to the phone and dialled. It took awhile before a gruff voice answered at the other end. The chief had been roused from an early sleep and wasn't at all pleased with the call. When the customs officer told him what was happening, however, his mood changed dramatically.

"I'll be right there," he promised, "and I'll take several men with me. Good thing the squad of men from the city is still in town."

In a surprisingly short time a troop of policemen was gathered in the police station. The chief, who was the first to come in, marched straight up to Tom and said, "Congratulations, my boy! You and Scout have done better than all the rest of us put together. I'm sorry I misjudged you."

Tom blushed. "I really didn't do much," he mumbled.

But the chief had already turned away from him to get more particulars from Barlinkhof and to draw up a plan of action.

CHAPTER XV

On the Stakeout

The conference between the chief and Barlinkhof did not take long. They decided that two men would accompany Barlinkhof, Tom, and Scout to the De Wit farm to catch the burglars. The others would immediately return to Falconhorst castle to pick up the men tied up in the underground chamber. Meanwhile, one man was dispatched to the Wentinck farm by bike in order to bring them the good news that Tom and Scout had been found.

A few moments later Sergeant Jansen drove up with the car. One of the policemen from the city, a huge fellow named Van Dyk, slid into the seat next to Jansen. Barlinkhof, Tom, and Scout climbed into the back seat. Then they sped off. The De Wit place was a long way out of town, but the car covered the distance in good time.

Suddenly Jansen put on the brakes. He had been driving with his headlights off as they neared the farm.

They were now standing on a narrow country road surrounded by trees. There were no buildings to be seen.

"Where is the place?" Tom asked quietly as they got out of the car.

"It's about a ten-minute walk from here," whispered Jansen. "If we go any farther by car, we might scare off the burglars. Maybe they're already inside. We have to move fast but without any noise. No talking from now on."

Swiftly, but with utmost care they hurried on. Jansen and Barlinkhof, who knew the way, were in the lead. The trees flitted by like dark phantoms. The night was cool, but Tom was shivering, not so much from the cold as from nerves. He had suffered a lot over the past two days.

As they rounded a bend in the road, suddenly the De Wit place came into view. The large white house looked elegant and peaceful in the moonlight. Jansen stopped and motioned to the others.

They put their heads close together, and he whispered very quietly, "From here on we have to be on our toes. We have to leave the road, so we'll lose the cover of the trees. We can't just walk up the driveway in this bright moonlight. But there's a drainage ditch that runs close to the farmhouse. That ditch is usually dry at this time of the year, so we'll creep up on the house that way."

He went on a few more metres until he came to the driveway leading to the farmhouse. Then he quietly lowered himself into the ditch. The others followed his example. Stooping low, they moved on, approaching very close to their goal without any problems.

Then Jansen gave them a hand signal to halt. He himself carefully crawled up the bank of the drainage ditch until he could peek over the side. The others waited in great suspense. It was a full five minutes before the sergeant moved again — five minutes that seemed like hours to Tom. Then Jansen looked back and whispered, "Come up here beside me."

In a moment Van Dyk, Barlinkhof, and Tom had also squirmed up the bank. The stately white house was bathed in moonlight. The trees and bushes in the yard threw back shadows. No light could be seen in the house, and there was no sign of the thieves.

"I've studied the place closely," whispered Jansen. "I think we got here in time and the burglars haven't made their move yet. There's a problem, however. We could hide in the bushes near the house, but then the watchdog will start barking. We could stay here, but this isn't a very ideal spot."

"I'm surprised the dog hasn't caught our scent here," Barlinkhof replied very quietly. "I know the animal. He's a strong beast and very alert."

"Where's the doghouse?"

"On this side of the house, behind those bushes. If I go down the ditch a little farther, I should be able to see the dog from there." Barlinkhof did as he had suggested. He slid back into the ditch and very carefully crept farther along the ditch. A few metres away he climbed up the bank again. He lay there, staring hard toward the house.

Five minutes later he was back. By the light of the moon, they could see the worried look on his face.

"There's something wrong," he whispered. "The dog is lying in front of the doghouse with his legs stretched straight out. I think he's dead." Again they conferred.

"I'm going to check and make sure," Jansen finally said.

He climbed up out of the ditch and swiftly moved in the direction of the doghouse. They watched him disappear behind the bushes.

Quite some time went by and still he hadn't reappeared. The threesome in the ditch were becoming uneasy. Had something happened to Jansen? Scout was the only one who didn't look worried; he lay beside Tom, his ears alertly pricked up.

All at once the shape of the tall sergeant again loomed up in the night, but from the opposite direction they had expected.

"Come on up," he whispered, "and I'll tell you what's up." Quickly they clambered up out of the ditch.

"Come on," he said. "We're right in the moonlight here. I don't like that."

He led them to the bushes alongside the farmhouse. When they had all concealed themselves, Jansen told them what he had found.

"The dog is dead," he said. "His body is stiff and swollen, so he must have been poisoned."

"Did those burglars do that?" asked Tom. He thought how awful he would feel if Scout were poisoned.

"I assume so," answered Jansen. "One of them must have come here earlier today to slip the dog a poisoned piece of meat or something. Those men stop at nothing, it seems. At first I was afraid they had already robbed the house too. So I went around the place and tried all the doors and examined the windows. I didn't see any signs of a break-in, so they must still be coming."

"We could hide ourselves in the house and jump them when they come in," suggested Van Dyk.

"If we had come a couple of hours earlier that would have been great," responded Jansen. "Then the old woman would still have been up. But now we would have to make too much noise to rouse her, and it would take too long for us to get settled inside. Chances are in the meantime we would have scared off the burglars, because they're probably not far away."

The others were forced to agree. Jansen sketched out another plan. He and Tom and Scout would stay in the bushes where they were while Van Dyk and Barlinkhof hid themselves in some bushes on the other side of the house. Then they would be able to spot the burglars no matter which side they came from.

The plan was put into action immediately. Van Dyk and Barlinkhof vanished around the house. Tom and Scout stayed with Jansen. The policeman seemed very calm, but Tom felt jittery. He kept seeing and hearing things, and then he would nudge Jansen to warn him. But every time it turned out to be a false alarm.

"Relax, Tom," the policeman said at last. "You've gone through a lot and have carried yourself bravely, but now you're letting your nerves get the better of you. Keep your eyes open, but don't allow yourself to get uptight. I'm sure Scout will let us know they're coming long before we see anything. Let Scout be your eyes and ears."

It happened exactly as Jansen had predicted. To the eyes of Jansen and Tom, the moonlit yard still lay peaceful and undisturbed when Scout suddenly began growling softly. The dog stared fiercely out into the field on the other side of the ditch.

The sergeant and Tom looked, but they saw nothing unusual. The field was dotted with small stacks of grain called shocks. The shocks gleamed in the moonlight, but nothing stirred in the field. They stared hard for a few minutes. Then Jansen whispered, "I don't see anything. Maybe Scout saw a dog or a cat out there."

But Tom shook his head. He knew Scout too well. The dog's hackles were up and a quiet, almost inaudible growl rose from deep in his throat. Scout had detected danger nearby.

Suddenly Jansen jerked forward in surprise. He pointed at the field and whispered, "Look, way at the other end of the field."

Tom looked in the direction the policeman was pointing. A dark shadow separated itself from one of the shocks and swiftly moved toward the farmhouse, immediately followed by a second shadow. In a few seconds they disappeared behind another shock of grain.

"Those are our boys all right!" whispered the policeman.

Scout was growling again, but Tom silenced him with a quiet command. The dog obeyed at once, but he kept his eyes fixed on the field.

In a few moments the two figures again darted out from behind the grain shocks. They were swiftly approaching the dry drainage ditch. Before they reached it, however, they vanished again. With taut nerves, the boy and the man hiding beside the house watched them come, and the dog, too, was on edge. A head appeared between two shocks and remained there, motionless, for several minutes. Apparently the thief was studying the farmhouse and the surroundings very closely to make sure everything was safe. Tom felt as if the man's eyes were looking right through the bushes where he was hiding. He was glad the sergeant and Scout were with him.

Then the head disappeared. They could hear the man talking quietly with his partner. The burglars had apparently concluded that the coast was clear, for they stepped out into the open and walked boldly to the ditch. They dropped out of sight for a minute and then came crawling up the bank on the side nearest the farmhouse and the bushes where Tom and his companions were hiding. The two men took a few more steps toward the house and then stopped.

Tom's heart was racing madly. If he reached forward between the branches, he could almost touch the nearest man. Again the two hoodlums whispered to each other.

"First I want to check out that dog," said one of them. "He's probably dead as a doornail after that juicy little treat I slipped him this afternoon."

The speaker brushed right by the bushes and disappeared in the direction of the doghouse. A moment later he was back: "He's taken care of, all right," he said with a chuckle. "He's stiff as a board already. He won't give us any trouble. Let's take a stroll around the house and check the place out first."

Although the men spoke very quietly, Jansen and Tom, who were about two metres away, understood every word.

When the two hoodlums had vanished around the corner of the house, Tom whispered, "Wouldn't it have been better if we had jumped them right away?" The sergeant shook his head. "We have to wait until they actually try to break in," he said. "Or else when they get in court, they'll simply deny everything and get away scot-free. Besides, now Barlinkhof and Van Dyk will know they're here, when they walk around the house."

Tom realized Jansen was right, but he was afraid the burglars would try to enter the house on the other side, and then he and Scout and Jansen would be left out of the action.

They waited in great suspense. The minutes dragged on. Tom was convinced the burglars were hitting the house from the other side, when the twosome suddenly appeared in the front again. They whispered together briefly and then padded silently to the side window of the living room. From his pocket, one of them took a tool with which he tried to pry up the window. Apparently he did not succeed. They heard him muttering in disgust. He put the tool away again and produced another one.

It was a glass cutter. Obviously the man knew how to use it. He pressed it against the window and with a soft squeal the instrument did its work. Meanwhile, his partner had taken out a large black cloth, which he spread on the ground and smeared with something from a can. Tom didn't understand what they were doing. The man pressed the cloth against the window, and a moment later they lifted away the window glass, almost soundlessly. One of the men swung his leg over the windowsill and started climbing inside.

"Now it's our turn," hissed Jansen, moving forward to the edge of the clump of bushes.

Tom cautiously crawled after him. Jansen waited a few more seconds, and then he leaped forward toward the window, followed by Tom and Scout.

The hoodlum standing outside the window was the first to see them. He shouted a warning to his buddy and then took to his heels. The other burglar frantically scrambled to get back outside, but he had no chance. Sergeant Jansen grabbed him. The man, however, was very strong and he put up a fierce fight. The sergeant was having trouble holding him, so Tom rushed in to give him a hand.

Tom and Jansen had their hands full trying to subdue the one man, so they were glad to see Barlinkhof and Van Dyk come running around the corner of the house. They rushed forward to help, but the sergeant shouted, "We'll hold this one. You two go after the other, or he'll get away!"

The two men hesitated a moment. They didn't know which way the man had fled, and the moon had just gone behind a cloud, so they could see nothing. Suddenly, however, they heard a scream of pain followed by angry snarls.

They immediately raced in the direction of the sounds. The men didn't have to see to know what had happened. Scout had

gone after the fleeing burglar and had sunk his teeth into him. When Van Dyk and Barlinkhof caught up to him, the hoodlum was lying on the ground with the German shepherd standing over him. The man hardly dared to move a muscle for fear the dog would go for his throat.

When they returned, triumphantly leading their prisoner, Jansen and Tom had also succeeded in subduing the other burglar. Waiting for just the right moment, when the man's resistance flagged for a second, Jansen had quickly snapped a pair of handcuffs on his wrists.

During all the commotion, the lights had come on in the farmhouse. The old woman had been wakened by the noise, and frightened half to death, she came shuffling to the window. The policemen quickly set her mind at ease and told her what had happened. She was visibly shaken to hear what a close call she had had and thanked the men repeatedly.

But Jansen was in a hurry to get going. "We have to get these prisoners to the police station as quickly as possible," he said. "The members of the gang picked up from the underground hideout should be there by now." Jansen said this purposely, and he saw the two men look up in shock when they heard the secret chamber had been discovered and the others also arrested. They had been acting proud and defiant, but now all the fight went out of them. They realized that the jig was up.

Leaving the prisoners to the care of his companions, Jansen trotted off to fetch the car. It wasn't long before Tom saw the yellow headlights turning up the long driveway.

A few minutes later the whole group was sitting in the car. One of the hoodlums was sitting in the front seat between Jansen and Barlinkhof, the other in the back between Van Dyk and Tom, while Scout sat on the floor between the seats. No one said much on the way back to the police station, but everyone except the two burglars was in a good mood.

Tom was tired, but happy. The mystery of Falconhorst castle had been solved and the smuggling ring captured. God had rescued him from sure death, and now he was returning safely to his family and friends. The warmth of the crowded car made him drowsy. Gradually he drifted off to sleep.

Tom didn't wake up until the car pulled to a stop. They were at the police station. Tom quickly jumped up. He was ashamed that he had dozed off while he should have been guarding the burglar. He hoped the others hadn't noticed. Apparently they hadn't. Jansen was the first one out of the car and then came everyone else. When they brought the two crooks into the station, they saw that the chief and the others were already back from the castle.

The chief was aglow with satisfaction and rubbed his hands in delight. He walked up to Tom and slapped him on the back. "We did it, my boy," he said jovially. "It was just as you said. We've booked the whole bunch of them and they're all sleeping in jail now. That sleeping potion must have been powerful. Now that you men have nabbed these other two I think we've got the whole gang behind bars. And we'd never have done it without your help. Thank you!"

Tom blushed. Now that the excitement was over, he felt exhausted. He didn't feel at all like a hero. All he wanted to do was go back to the farm, to Ina and Miriam and all the others who must be sitting up waiting for him.

The chief seemed to have read his thoughts, for he called Jansen and said, "I think you'd better bring our young detective and his dog back to the Wentincks as quickly as possible. Take the car. They've carried themselves bravely, but I think it's high time they got a little rest."

"All right if I ride along?" asked Barlinkhof. "I don't have anything more to do around here anyway. Yesterday I saw all those gloomy faces at the Wentincks, now I want to see what they look like when Tom comes back."

When they arrived at the farm, Wentinck was already standing out in the yard. But before the car came to a halt, Mrs. Wentinck, Jake, Hanna, Ina, Miriam, Carl, and Bert also came storming out of the house. The girls threw their arms about him, sobbing with joy, and his friends grabbed his hands and shook them. They were overjoyed to see him alive and well again, for they had thought him dead.

Triumphantly Tom and Scout were escorted inside. Jansen and Barlinkhof were also invited in.

About an hour before, Wentinck had been woke up by a policeman, who had told him that Tom was safe. First he had decided to let the other children sleep, but he had been unable to keep the good news to himself. Besides, he knew they wouldn't sleep well as long as they were still worried about Tom. So he had awoken them all. In no time they had all jumped into their clothes to await the return of Tom and Scout.

The room hummed with joy. After a little while Jansen and Barlinkhof said goodbye and drove back into town. The young people were bursting with curiosity about Tom's adventures and wanted Tom to tell them everything. But Mrs. Wentinck said firmly, "Nothing doing. Tom is going straight to bed and get some rest before he does anything else; otherwise he'll get sick. We can hear the story later."

The others were a little disappointed, but they knew Mrs. Wentinck was right. And Tom, who was glowing with happiness, but who was also blinking with sleepiness end exhaustion, was inwardly glad to be going straight to bed.

He had hardly finished pulling up the covers before he was asleep. His faithful, four-footed companion curled up beside his bed and also settled down for a snooze.

It was evening before Tom vaguely became aware that someone was in the room with him. He felt a hand on his forehead and lips on his cheek. He struggled up out of the grip of deep sleep and opened his eyes. His mother was bending over him. She was crying and laughing at the same time and showered him with kisses.

Tom's father, too, was standing by the bed, obviously struggling to control his emotions.

Tom was now wide awake. He sat up and stared at his parents in surprise. "How . . . how did you get here?" he stammered, dumbfounded.

"Mr. Wentinck called us," said Father, laughing. "We were so glad to hear you had been saved from terrible danger, we hopped into the car and drove down."

Tom jumped out of bed and quickly dressed himself, while Scout, infected by his master's excitement, pranced around him, barking and wagging his tail.

Together they went downstairs. The Wentincks were sitting on the bench in front of the house enjoying the beautiful evening, and their guests lay in the grass under the big red birch. They were all glad to see Mr. and Mrs. Sanders.

Now Tom had to tell them about his adventures. The children especially were burning with curiosity about what had happened to him. Quietly and without dramatics, he told them everything.

He admitted that he had done wrong in taking off in the canoe without telling anyone. When he told the story of the discovery of the underground passage, his capture by the smugglers, and his escape with the help of the gypsy, the young people hung on his every word, while the adults, too, listened in growing amazement.

When he was finally finished, a chorus of voices broke loose. His friends and sisters were full of questions and wanted to know more and more. Tom's mother was pale and had tears in her eyes. Only now did she realize in what danger her boy had been.

Mr. Sanders put a hand on Tom's shoulder. "You should have been more careful," he said, "although you carried yourself well later on. It certainly wasn't due to your cleverness that everything turned out well. God saved you. Did you remember to thank Him for it?" Tom nodded. He had prayed fervently for rescue when he was in danger, and he had also thanked God for safely bringing him back.

CHAPTER XVI

Return to the Scene

The days that followed were especially pleasant. Mr. Sanders had arranged to take off several days from work. The children had twice as much fun now that Tom and Ina's parents were there too. They made numerous tours about the area, and of course, the children had to show Mr. and Mrs. Sanders all the beautiful spots they had discovered.

On one of their first outings, they looked for Wasil's trailer. But it was gone. Apparently he had done as he had told Tom.

"Too bad," said Mr. Sanders. "I would have liked to thank the man. He may have done wrong, but he did save our boy's life."

Soon further news arrived about the members of the smuggling ring. The newspapers carried extensive stories of the gang's capture and arrest. Some of the stories were written with a great deal of imagination. They gave the group at the Wentinck farm many a laugh.

Barlinkhof and Jansen, who stopped in every once in a while, also brought them many newspaper clippings. At the same time, they also brought confidential bits of news about the trial of the gang.

Once the chief himself even stopped in. He wanted to thank Tom one more time and again apologize for his earlier skepticism. Now that he had become good friends with the young people, he turned out to be a very engaging character after all. He was an excellent storyteller and told the guests many incidents that had happened in this part of the country over the last few years.

At first the questioning of the smugglers had met with little success. No one admitted to anything. All of them were apparently afraid of the leader. Gradually, however, the chief pried a few details loose from a couple of the men and then played them all off against each other. Once they got the idea that everything had been spilled anyway, the chief was flooded with confessions.

The German commander, who was the leader of the smuggling ring, had been stationed in this part of the country during the war. He had been the commander of an S.S. unit which had planted landmines near Falconhorst castle. His troops had camped in the ancient ruins for some time.

He had heard the old story of Ada's escape from the besieged tower and had immediately suspected that there was a secret passage. On his own he had begun a search of the place and had found the blue stone by accident. But he had guarded the secret very carefully in order to make use of it later.

After the end of the war, the S.S. officer, afraid of prosecution for war crimes, had gone into hiding. Then he had remembered the secret of Falconhorst and conceived the plan to use the secret passage in a profitable smuggling operation. So he had contacted some of his former S.S. underlings, among them several Dutch S.S. men, who came in very handy because they could move about freely in the Netherlands. The gang had secretly established its headquarters in the underground chamber. The Dutch members of the gang had made contacts with smugglers and black market dealers in their country, and the Germans had done the same on their side of the border. All had been sworn to the strictest secrecy, under penalty of death.

The minefields planted around the castle ruins fit right into the smugglers' plans. It kept almost everyone away from the castle. Actually the land mines had secretly been removed one night by some of the gang. The S.S. officer had a map of the minefield, so he knew exactly where they had been placed. The explosives had been saved for use in their planned burglaries. This was why Tom and Scout had been able to cross the field unhurt.

The role that Wasil had played in the operation agreed closely with what the old gypsy himself had told Tom.

In the underground chamber and several other underground cells the police found a large stock of smuggled goods. The silverware stolen from the Rykenhoek mansion was also still there, as well as many other valuables collected on other break-ins.

So the police had made an unusually big haul. No less pleased than the police were the customs officials. Finally the mystery of how such large amounts of goods could get across the border undetected in this area had been solved. The goods weren't taken over the border but under it, through the underground passage that opened in Germany. So the local customs officers had been cleared of all suspicion that they were in cahoots with the smugglers. This made Barlinkhof and his fellow officers very happy.

The publicity of the last few days and the discovery of the underground passages attracted many sightseers to the area. But because the case was not yet closed, the police placed the ruins off-limits to sightseers.

This deeply disappointed Tom's companions, for they would dearly have loved to see the underground room and to walk through the underground passages. When they were brooding about this one day, Jake suddenly said with a straight face, "I'll fix it with the chief."

The others laughed at him. "Listen to the big shot!" Carl teased.

But Jake didn't back down. "You'll see. The chief will fix it up for us," he said as he went out the door back to work.

The others thought he had been joking, but the following day Jake came home with a letter giving the Wentincks and their guests permission to tour the ruins and the underground passages in the company of Jansen and Barlinkhof. When Jake read the letter out loud, a noisy cheer went up. He told them he had simply gone to the police station and told the chief that Tom's friends and parents would very much like to see the place where Tom and Scout had spent so many anxious hours.

The chief, who had been in an exceptionally good mood since the arrest of the smugglers, had immediately granted them permission. And Jake had jumped at the opportunity to get permission for himself and his family to see the tunnels at the same time. "You see," he said seriously, but with a twinkle in his eyes, "the chief knew he couldn't let a bunch of innocent young children go down into that spooky underground room by themselves. Who knows, maybe there are still gang members hiding down there in some dark corner. So he sent me along to protect you."

Again Jake was jeered for being a blowhard, but the group was only too grateful for what he had done. The grown-ups were no less pleased at the prospect of seeing the ruins.

They went that same afternoon, accompanied by Sergeant Jansen and Mr. Barlinkhof. When they reached the edge of the minefield, they saw a policeman just turning back a group of strangers who had come to explore the ruins on their own. They waited until the disappointed sightseers had left and then showed the guard their letter. He waved them on without asking any questions.

The ancient ruins lay gray and sombre in the bright sunlight, and the dark, weather-beaten tower rose up imposingly. The stone falcon above the crumbling gateway looked down on them as mysteriously as ever. It did not seem to be aware that the secret of Falconhorst castle had been found out.

The party crossed the court and walked through the collapsed halls and corridors until they reached the tower. The door grated on its hinges as Jake opened it. Everyone stepped inside.

Although it was midday, the tower room was steeped in a mysterious twilight. They had had a long, hot walk and sat down on the stone benches for a few minutes to catch their breath in the cool interior. Again the young people felt the strange pull of the past, which they had also felt when Jake had told them the story of Lord Ewald and his daughter Ada.

Jake probably felt the same, for he quietly began to speak. "When I told you about the mystery of the castle, I didn't know everything. Through Tom's adventures we can fill in the blanks. When Ada had said goodby to her dying father, she withdrew herself into this room with her remaining servants. They securely locked the door.

"While the helpers of Black Bertram tried to break open the door of the tower, one of the servants walked to the blue stone and pressed it. Ada and her servants escaped through the open trapdoor. From below they closed the door again.

"While the roaring Black Bertram jumped inside with a burning torch and looked around for his prey, the fugitives were in the underground room. From there they must have escaped through the tunnel Tom discovered."

"That's probably how it went," said Mr. Wentinck. "But now it's time for us to go and have a look downstairs."

Barlinkhof stood up and pressed the blue stone. The trapdoor opened so suddenly, the children started in fright. One by one they lowered themselves onto the stairs leading into the darkness. A little later the whole party was standing in the underground chamber.

Jansen and Barlinkhof as well as Tom had taken along powerful flashlights. The table and chairs of the smuggling ring were still there. The two cabinets were standing open and empty. They had contained part of the loot collected during their break-ins.

Once again Tom told his friends and family how he had tumbled into the room, pointing out the door, how the fight had gone, which chair he had sat on, and so on. In this setting the story made an even greater impression than before. The young people shuddered when they saw the cell in which Tom had been imprisoned, and the grownups seemed to feel the walls closing in on them.

After looking everything over, the group took a walk down the tunnel leading to the island. Even though they had flashlights, they felt a vague fear as they followed each other down the long, dark passage. Thanks to the smugglers, Jansen had learned how to work the mechanism that closed off the entrance from inside the tunnel. When they came to the stone stairway, he pushed hard on something, and a few moments later daylight filtered down the eroded steps. When the group was outside, the stone platform slowly lifted them up into the clearing between the bushes. They all breathed in relief when they emerged in the sunlight.

The smugglers' boat still lay in the same spot between the tall reeds. "We may as well take it along right now," said Jansen. "It may serve as evidence during the trial, and in any case it shouldn't stay here."

The boat was quite large so everyone in the party fit in it at the same time. Wentinck picked up the large pole and pushed the craft out of the reeds. Then Jake, Carl, Tom, and Bert each took an oar and rowed across the Black Pool in the direction of town. At first their rowing went somewhat clumsily and gave rise to gales of laughter, for a spray of water went over the boat every time the boys missed a stroke. But soon they caught on and were rowing in unison.

When they reached the spot where the river came nearest the village, Jansen said, "Let's beach the boat here. The chief can decide what to do with it from here."

The Wentincks and their guests said goodbye to the sergeant and the customs officer and hiked home together. The young people were still deeply affected by their tour through the mysterious underground hideout. Although they had been thrilled to see it, now they were happy to be back in the open air. For the first time, they realized how harrowing Tom and Scout's adventures had really been.

Not long after the visit to the ruins, Mr. and Mrs. Sanders left for *Heathview* again. The young people were staying a few more days. They enjoyed themselves tremendously, but they discovered that fame has certain drawbacks. They could hardly go anywhere without becoming the centre of attention.

Nevertheless, they all agreed that this had been the best vacation any of them had ever had. And on the last day, when Mr. Wentinck invited the whole group to come again next year, they answered with one voice, "SURE!"

"When you come back next summer," said Wentinck, "Falconhorst castle will look very different. I just heard that the ruins are going to be restored as much as possible and that the whole place, including the underground room, will be opened to the public. It should attract a lot of tourists to this area. I think they'll probably close the tunnel leading into Germany. Otherwise that might prove to be something of a headache." The children found it hard to say goodbye, but they were already looking forward to next summer. They thanked the Wentincks enthusiastically for their hospitality.

Jake had already hitched up the horses. This time they rode to the railroad station in the buggy. Jake accompanied them onto the platform and waited with them until the train came chugging into the station. Everyone in the group shook hands with him and then climbed into an empty compartment. The station master gave the signal, and, trembling and wheezing, the locomotive slowly picked up speed again.

For a little while the five youngsters could wave to Jake, but then the tracks curved and he disappeared from view.

"Too bad it's over," sighed Ina. And the others nodded their agreement.

"But next year we can come again, Scout," said Tom, scratching his dog's head. "And maybe then there will be new adventures waiting for us." Wagging his tail happily, Scout barked his approval.

And although he couldn't talk, he expressed the feeling of the whole group.

Young Burning Hearts Series

The Young Burning Hearts Series is a series of fascinating independent stories for young and old of faithfulness in trying times.

The Little Captives **by Deborah Alcock**
A Story of the Fourth Century

The trembling little captives soon found themselves in the presence of the barbarian king. He sat on a raised seat, or throne, conspicuous among the dusky crowd that surrounded him by the rich adornments of his dress, and the staff, or sceptre, which he held in his hand.

Time: about AD 400 **Age: 12-99**
ISBN 978-1-77298-017-2 **US$7.90**

A Child's Victory **by Deborah Alcock**
A Story of the Twelfth Century

On a sultry summer's day, in the twelfth century, a little girl stood at a street door in one of the close, narrow alleys of a Flemish town. Her dress indicated poverty, though not neglect. Other children were playing near; she heard their voices, and looked at them for a few moments with curiosity and interest in her large blue eyes, but apparently with no wish to join their sports. Far more earnestly did she gaze to the right, where the long alley terminated in a broader street, from which a stream of intensely vivid sunlight poured, illuminating a corner of the shaded alley, with the Madonna in her niche, as well as the quaint carvings that adorned the house of rich Master Andreas the weaver. What would little Arlette have given to see one figure that she knew turn from the sunshine into the shadow!

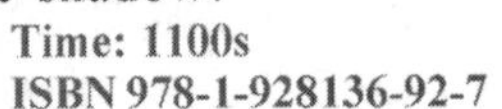
Time: 1100s
ISBN 978-1-928136-92-7

Age: 12-99
US$7.90

The Story of a Poor Scholar by Deborah Alcock

A Story about Germany and Bohemia

"Indeed?" said the old man, his face lighting up with sympathy and interest. "We have heard of the people who are called Brethren of the Unity, or United Brethren, and we own them as brethren indeed, in Christ Jesus our Lord — whose Gospel they knew and honoured, and whom they served and died for, many years before the voice of Dr. Martin Luther was heard in this Saxon land of ours."

"And we also," Wenzel responded, "we honour the name of your great teacher, Dr. Luther, whom God raised up to show His pure Evangel to the people of Germany, even as, one hundred years before, He sent us our dear and venerated Master John Huss. That is why I am going now to Wittenberg, to pursue my studies there."

Time: 1550s **Age: 12-99**

ISBN 978-1-928136-96-5 **US$7.90**

The Martyr of Kolin by H.O. Ward

A Story of the Bohemian Persecution

When I reached home from afternoon school, I went up to a little upper chamber which Wilma and I had as our own, and there I found my sister — who was at the time a fair young maiden of thirteen — busy with her needle.

"Well, Sister," said I, "so we are to have another of these good gentlemen tonight."

"He has come," she said mysteriously.

"Has he? What is he like?" I asked.

"I have not seen him, for he is closeted with our father in his private chamber."

"Will he sup openly with us tonight?"

"Yes, I think so. Elspeth will keep a careful watch, and there is the door behind the tapestry, you know, in case of a surprise."

Time: 1560-1580 **Age: 12-99**

ISBN 978-1-928136-47-7 **US$12.90**

The Martyr's Widow **by Deborah Alcock**

A Story About The Netherlands

"Flee, Carl! Oh, flee while you can!"

"It is too late! Where should I flee to?"

Another loud impatient knock, and a sound of rough voices outside.

But a thought, sent as she believed from Heaven into her heart, inspired Lisa with sudden hope and courage. She seized her husband by the arm, and drew him toward the little closet, the door of which she had left open.

"There — in there — fear nothing — I will speak to them."

Time: 1570s **Age: 12-99**

ISBN 978-1-77298-000-4 **US$7.90**

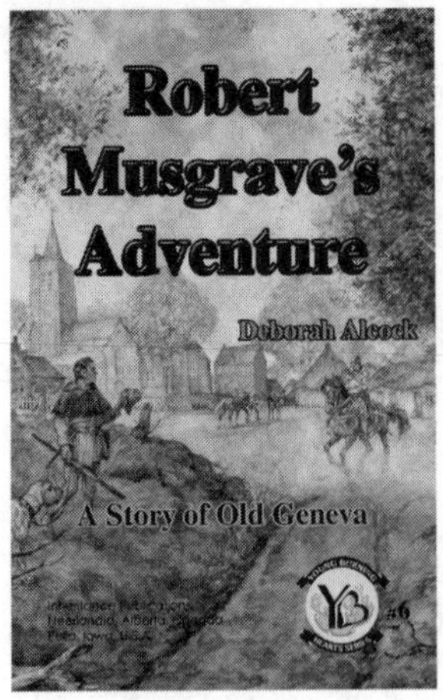

Robert Musgrave's Adventure
by Deborah Alcock
A Story of Old Geneva

"Josef . . . the servant, ye know," said Jeannot, "told us how the soldiers of Captain Brunaulieu's corps, as they came to a halt outside the town, found amongst them a boy who was evidently a Genevan. They seized him, and brought him to the Captain. He said he was an Englishman, which, I suppose, is another kind of heretic . . . oh, I crave pardon of your Worthinesses . . ."

"Never mind our Worthinesses, but go on with thy story," said someone.

"The Captain would have had him run through at once. But the holy Friar who was with them — Friar Alexander the Scotchman, they called him — bade spare him, as he might be of use in the town for a guide. 'Twas just then that Josef, who told us the tale, came up, being sent on a message . . ."

Time: 1602 **Age: 12-99**

ISBN 978-1-928136-32-3 **US$8.90**

Sunset in Provence by Deborah Alcock
A Tale of the Albigenses

"My lord, I am your sister's son but not your vassal," the youth replied with perhaps unnecessary pride. "But that is not the question," he added sadly and in a gentler tone. "You counsel me — no, you command me," and he bowed his head slightly at the word, "to submit myself unreservedly to our Holy Father the Pope, in the person of his Legate."

"I do, as you do value life and lands. If your retainers had not infected you with their heresy, why should you hesitate?"

"I — the son of Roger Taillefer — a heretic! None of our race were ever that, thank Heaven. But can the Count ask why I hesitate? Not that I fear the disgrace of a public penance, though I think they might have spared it to the greatest seigneur who speaks the 'Langue d'Oc', and altogether such a submissive and obedient Roman Catholic."

Time: 1200s **Age: 12-99**

ISBN 978-1-928136-94-1 **US$7.90**

The Cloak in Pledge by Deborah Alcock
A Story About Russia

"If we only had something better for the little one," Ivan added, in a lower tone. "He can't eat that."

"Don't fret, Father," said Michael, a good-humoured lad on the whole. "I'll ask Master to give me a roll for him at dinner-time, and besides, there's Peter —" (the brother next in age, who had just got a place as one of the boy-postillions the wealthy Russians were so fond of having) — "Peter may come and see us, and bring us a kopeck or two for him."

Time: 1800s **Age: 12-99**

ISBN 978-1-928136-95-8 **US$7.90**

Archie's Chances **by Deborah Alcock**
A Story of the Nineteenth Century

This was scarcely as bad as she expected, yet quite bad enough. She flushed hotly. "Uncle has not said anything to you, has he?" she asked.
"Never once. Kate, Uncle Morris is a brick!" There was a wealth of genuine gratitude flung into the boyish word that redeemed it from all trace of vulgarity.
"If Father were alive, what would he say?" questioned Kate. "I think he would be horrified at the very thought."
"Well, I don't know," mused Archie, thrusting his hands into his pockets. "After all, the horrible thing is eating the shop — I mean the bread that's made in it. And since I do that already, and can't help myself, I think it would not make things any worse to earn it before I eat it."

Time: 1880s **Age: 12-99**
ISBN 978-1-894666-16-9 **US$8.90**

Truth Stranger Than Fiction **by Deborah Alcock**
The King of Hungary's Blacksmith
and other Stories

"Well, Master Jailer, how goes it? Have you heard anything?" asked the young man in an eager whisper.
The jailer laid his hand compassionately on his shoulder. "Heavy tidings for thee, poor lad," he said. "He will likely die."
The answer was a deep groan, heard distinctly through all the uproar of the crowded room. Then silence; then a broken murmur, "Poor Maida — poor baby!" choked by something very like the suppressed sob of a strong man.

Time: 1570s **Age: 12-99**
ISBN 978-1-77298-001-1 **US$7.90**

Etchings from History **by Deborah Alcock**
Illustrating the Proverbs of Solomon

After a brief though brilliant career (in which he rendered important political services to the cause of Protestantism), Maurice was killed in the battle of Sievershausen, in his thirty-second year. He had enjoyed his electorate about five years. His brother succeeded him, for his only son had died before him. One little daughter, Anna, survived him. She was afterward married, with great pomp and show, to the celebrated William the Silent, Prince of Orange.

Time: 1570s **Age: 12-99**
ISBN 978-1-928136-97-2 **US$7.90**

Strangers in the Valleys **by Deborah Alcock**
A Continuation of *Sunset in Provence*

"Listen! Someone knocks."

Henri sprang to the door, and hastily unbarred it. A young man, whose fur coat was covered with snow, entered immediately, bringing a current of cold air and a stream of water into the comfortable room.

"You here, Christophe!" cried the pastor, recognizing a member of his flock who lived at a considerable distance. "What errand has brought you so far on such a night?"

"An ill one, Barbe," said the young man. "My poor mother — God help her! — lies since morning speechless, and as far as I can see, at the point of death."

It must be remembered that the barbe was by his calling a physician for the body as well as for the soul. It was not necessary, therefore, for the young peasant even to express a desire that he should accompany him. Without a moment's delay he rose to prepare for the expedition. It was a difficult, toilsome, and even dangerous one. A walk of seven miles at night, and in a snow-storm . . .

Time: 1200s **Age: 12-99**

ISBN 978-1-77298-026-4 **US$9.90**

YBH13 The First Campaign of Arnold Viersen by Ronald Van Reest

"It sure feels good," said Arnold, "driving an old car to start my first campaign. That's how many politicians have done it.""Indeed," said Ronald, thinking of a story about the well-known preacher, Robert Schuller of Crystal Cathedral in California. Apparently, Rev. Schuller and his wife had begun their ministry, travelling in an old Volkswagenbus. They would park it at a street corner and he preached from the roof of the bus. Rev. Schuller was not known for orthodoxy, but his humble beginnings were certainly worthy of admiration. "So this is your first campaign trip?""Yes, apart from going door to door. I have signed up more than two hundred people locally. But several hundred more will be needed in order to win the nomination. Tony Van Pater said that if he had had three hundred more supporters, he would have won his nomination."

Time: 2015 Age: 12-99

ISBN 978-1-77298-034-9 US$7.90